Everybody's
Somebody's
Fool

Also by Ed Gorman

The Sam McCain Series
The Day the Music Died • *Wake Up Little Susie* • *Will You Still Love Me Tomorrow?* • *Save the Last Dance for Me*

The Jack Dwyer Series
New, Improved Murder • *Murder Straight Up* • *Murder in the Wings* • *The Autumn Dead* • *A Cry of Shadows*

The Tobin Series
Murder on the Aisle • *Several Deaths Later*

The Robert Payne Series
Blood Moon • *Hawk Moon* • *Harlot's Moon*

Suspense Novels
The Night Remembers • *The First Lady* • *Runner in the Dark* • *Senatorial Privilege*

Short Story Collections
Prisoners • *Dark Whispers* • *Moonchasers*

Everybody's Somebody's Fool

ED GORMAN

CARROLL & GRAF PUBLISHERS
NEW YORK

Everybody's Somebody's Fool

Carroll & Graf Publishers
An Imprint of Avalon Publishing Group Inc.
161 William St., 16th Floor
New York, NY 10038

First Carroll & Graf edition 2002

Library of Congress Cataloging-in-Publication Data is available.

ISBN: 0-7867-1114-0

Printed in the United States of America
Distributed by Publishers Group West

For the good doctors Tammy O'Brien, M.D.; Dean H. Gesme Jr., M.D., F.A.C.P.; Kevin Carpenter, M.D., F.A.C.S.; Leann Schneider, LPN; that very special oncology nurse Amy Hass; and the lovely ladies of the lab—Carolyn, Denise, Marcia, Sherry, and Wendy.

And hearts that we broke long ago
Have long been breaking others.
                              —W. H. Auden

Everybody's
Somebody's
Fool

PART I

ONE

AROUND ELEVEN THAT NIGHT, the hostess broke out the Johnny Mathis and the Frank Sinatra, and everybody quit talking about their kids and their jobs and their mortgages and their politics, and got down to some serious slow dancing out on the darkened patio in the warm prairie night of summer 1961.

It was like all those groping, grasping ninth-grade parties we'd always had in some kid's basement, where the mom was gracious and the old man cast an evil eye on anybody who danced too close with his sweet blooming daughter.

The difference now was that we were adults, or rumored to be, or hoped devoutly to be. Andre Malraux once asked an old priest if he'd learned anything from sixty years of hearing confessions and the padre said, "Yes, there's no such thing as an adult." He was probably on to something there.

There were only three single women there that night, and only one single guy. Me.

I took turns dancing with all three of them and all three of them said pretty much the same thing when I slid into their embrace, "Gosh, McCain, you always make me feel so tall." And then a giggle.

There's nothing worse than being insulted by people who don't mean to insult you. At five-five a guy can be awfully sensitive about short jokes.

We danced.

Back in high school the only girl I wanted to dance with was the beautiful Pamela Forrest, the girl I'd loved since grade school. But since she went out with older boys, I didn't get to dance with her very often.

As I saw it, my prospective dancing partners were divided into three groups. Girls who were shorter than I was and therefore good for my public image; girls who were fun to dance with no matter how short or tall they were; and girls who didn't mind a little dry-humping in the darkness. There weren't many in the last category, at least not many available to me, anyway, but when you came upon one you immediately fell to your knees sobbing in gratitude.

Tonight, I was hoping I'd find a girl who, at twenty-five, had moved beyond the dry-humping stage. The best bet was Linda Dennehy, who was divorced and worked as a nurse in Iowa City, well known to be the capital of all great-looking girls in our state. I mean, you had girls there who'd been to Paris and London walking around in heartbreaking Levi cut-offs openly reading Kerouac and Ginsberg. I spent as much time there as I could.

Linda was a little bit drunk and a little bit sentimental. She smelled good, too. Very good. "You ever wish you could go back, Sam, you know, to when we were in high school?"

"All the time."

"I thought it was going to be so neat. You know, growing up and going out on my own."

I paid all the attention I could. The feel of her flesh beneath her silk blouse and silk slip made certain parts of my body more alert than others. There was a bonus to her slender but very female form. I liked her. Always had. She was one of those quiet, decent girls who, oddly enough, looked better with eyeglasses than without them. Nobody paid a lot of attention to her back then is what I'm trying to say. But on hayrack rides and at skating parties and on Fourth of July starburst keggers, we'd drifted together sometimes, friends and maybe a little more, but never enough little more that it ever went anywhere.

"You still have your ragtop?"

"I sure do."

"I don't suppose you'd feel like going for a ride?"

"I sure would."

"I have to tell you something, though."

She didn't finish the sentence, leaving me to wonder what she wanted to say but didn't quite have the courage to. (A) I have to tell you, though, that I'm three months preggers. (B) I have to tell you, though, that I somehow picked up a venereal disease. (C) I have to tell you, though, that if I meet somebody who's taller than you, I'm going to dump you in a minute.

"Tell me what?"

She put her arm around my neck and kissed me. She had a very soft mouth and a very deft tongue and I have to say that I went a wee bit cuckoo standing there on that patio. Not only hadn't I had sex in some time, I hadn't had any companionship. And right now in that shadowy darkness, I felt as if Linda was the best friend I'd ever had.

"God, I can't believe I did that, Sam."

"You don't hear me complaining, do you?"

"It's—embarrassing." She glanced about. A few of the other couples had taken note of our kiss.

The song ended.

"I need to go to the bathroom first," she said. "Will you wait here?"

"I'm nailed to the floor."

I watched her walk away, a pleasing sight indeed. Slender but not without some elemental curves. We'd grown up in the Knolls together. That's the section that the proper citizens of Black River Falls try to forget about. A lot of tiny, rusty shacks and hundreds of scrubby little kids doomed to live out the same kind of grim, gray lives of their parents and enough violence to inspire the day-dreams of a dozen generals.

Even by Knolls standards, Linda's father was a bastard. My dad and a lot of other dads took turns hauling his drunken ass off his fragile little wife, whom he seemed to enjoy beating up on the front lawn of their shacklike house. When he was very drunk, it'd take a couple of dads—maybe even three of them—to put the monster down because he was not only big, he'd once been a good amateur fighter.

Linda would hurl herself upon him, screaming, literally tearing hair out of his head, scratching his eyes, biting his shoulder—anything to stop him from smashing punches again and again into her tiny mother. On summer nights, long after her old man had been laid low by one of the dads and lay passed out on the front stoop, I could hear Linda crying into the night. She couldn't seem to stop herself. If she had friends, I never saw them or heard about them. She liked to fish, God did she like to fish, and growing up, before my dad started making enough money to move us into town proper, I always saw her down on that old deserted railroad bridge, so solitary in her T-shirt and jeans it'd break your heart that way your little sister could break your heart. And if you approached her, she'd jump up and run away.

Her father was dead now and her two younger brothers were driving for a trucking company. She'd gotten a scholarship to nursing school and had done well for herself. Her drinking tonight surprised me. The few times I'd seen her at social affairs she'd always made a point of drinking nonalcoholic things.

I went over and poured myself a little bit of nonalcoholic punch myself. My dad and I share the same ability to get absolutely stoned on three cans of 3.2 beer, so I generally stay away from alcohol.

A hot August breeze came and ruffled all the pines that surrounded this expensive fashion plate of a house. Two vast stories done in a mock-Plantation style. The Coyles' house. Jack Coyle was a lawyer who'd inherited a good deal of money when his father, also a lawyer, died recently. He'd also inherited the family manse. In a town of 27,000 like Black River Falls, the Coyles passed for royalty. They were nice, unassuming folk with a pair of twin girls everybody said should be in TV commercials, they were so damned cute.

I didn't like Jack Coyle. In the old days I would've felt class anger. He'd gone back east to school—Yale—and clerked for a Supreme Court justice and had come back here to become the dominant lawyer of his generation. He was in his early forties. He'd had all the breaks.

My class resentment aside, I didn't like him for a specific reason. A few years ago, when I set up my own practice, I asked him if I might drop by and ask him some questions. He was nice enough—his wife and I were longtime school friends—until a secretary walked by his open door. He stopped talking to me and snapped at her to get in there.

She came in, all right, and he laid into her with the fury of a drunken brawler. This was 11 A.M. and he was quite sober. She'd forgotten to give him a message—or she'd garbled a message she'd given him—I could never figure out which it was.

Right in front of me, he ripped into her not only professionally but personally. How stupid she was. How slow she was. How irresponsible she was. And how fat she'd gotten. How her clothes always looked sloppy on her. And how irritating it was that she was always running off to the john.

And I had to sit there pretending to be invisible and deaf.

His rage seemed endless. And her inevitable tears—every once in a while she'd glance at me in her shame and humiliation—only seemed to make him angrier.

No matter how she'd let him down, she didn't deserve to be treated like this. And especially with me sitting there.

When it was over, he said, "What a stupid cow of a bitch. Five years ago she was a good-looking woman. Then she had two kids and let herself go. That's what I should do with her—let her go. I'm just too damned softhearted."

I almost laughed out loud. I mean, given what he'd just done to that poor woman—and he could still see himself as "softhearted." He was about as softhearted as Himmler.

But here I was drinking his liquor. I leaned against the patio wall, watching the dancers and remembering them as they'd been when we were all in school together, remarking to myself on all the usual ironies of why the A student was still a bag boy and how fate or the gods had conspired to turn the portly drab girl into a knockout babe and what kind of small but significant social courage it must take for the guy with the clubfoot to get out there and dance, fast or slow, without ever seeming self-conscious, and to hell with what anybody might think.

A fragile hand touched my arm. Jean Coyle. Somewhat prim but very pretty. She'd been our class valedictorian. She wore a dark cocktail dress and had short dark hair. She was one of those women who could look dressed up in a work shirt and worn jeans. She was the good catch of her generation in our valley—good family, good education, a socially skilled wife for a prominent man. Jack Coyle was fifteen years her senior. But his powerful presence—he had a kind of tanned country club virility, and the graying traces of black Irish hair only added to it somehow—narrowed the age difference.

"Hi, Sam."

"Hi, Jean. I was going to look you up before I left, to thank you for tonight. I had a good time."

"Thank you, Sam. I hope everybody did."

I nodded to the dance floor. Everybody was in passionate embrace. "Sure looks like it."

"I wonder if you'd come with me for a little bit."

Some women might have made a naughty joke of the request. Jean wasn't the type. If she wanted you to go somewhere with her, it was for a perfectly legitimate reason.

Just then, Linda came back.

She thanked Jean, who looked uncomfortable with Linda suddenly. "Would you mind if Sam helped me with something for a few minutes?"

"No. Not at all."

"Be right back," I said.

Linda touched my arm. "I'm looking forward to that ride." The way she touched my arm, portending all sorts of things, was far sexier than if she'd kissed my neck. It was sweet and sexy at the same time. It's never fun to realize what a pitiful grasping creature I am. She touched my arm and my Midwestern mind was rhapsodic with romance.

As Jean led me through the elegant house that just missed being a bit too showy, she said, "I hate to drag you into this, Sam. I was going to call Cliffie but he's such an idiot."

I laughed. "Our Cliffie? The chief of police? I guess I never noticed that he was an idiot."

Her smile was forced.

We went out the front door and around the side of the house. There was a white gazebo on the west edge of the lawn. It glowed in the moonlight.

"This is getting pretty mysterious," I laughed.

"It shouldn't be. It's in your line of work, Sam. You have a private investigator's license and everything, I mean."

"What kind of work is it, Jean?"

She said, "There's a dead girl in the gazebo."

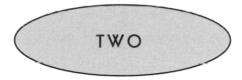

TWO

THE GAZEBO CONFORMED TO the classic pattern, octagonal in shape, fretted with Victorian touches, and just wide enough to hold a glider and two sitting chairs comfortably.

Jean had brought a small flashlight along and handed it to me just before we reached the gazebo.

The girl, who was familiar to me in some way, was tucked into a corner of the glider. She was dressed sorority girl–style, black flats, a dark wrap-around skirt closed with a large golden safety pin, a summery white blouse. Death was obvious but not disfiguring. Though her dark-haired head was pitched at an uncomfortable angle on her shoulder, her posture was perfect, even prim.

The eyes were closed. She'd possessed the kind of austere, important beauty that only the rich boys and the top jocks had a chance with. She had the looks of all the ethereal troubled girls in F. Scott Fitzgerald novels. I imagined she was twenty.

The wound was on the side of her head, the blood lost in the texture of the hair. I didn't want to touch her to see how wide and deep the wound went. Blunt instrument trauma, presumably.

I said, "We need to call Cliffie."

"He's such a boob."

"Yeah, he is. But he's also the chief of police and this is a crime scene."

"The Griffins are such nice people."

"The Griffins? He's got the Cadillac dealership?"

"Yes. You mean you don't know who the girl is? It's their daughter, Sara."

"That's who she is. Was she invited to the party tonight?"

"Lord, no, Sam. She's a sophomore in college. Way too young for our crowd." She bit her lip. "I just wonder what she was doing here."

"Did you tell Jack?"

"I haven't had a chance yet."

"How did you find her?"

She made a perfectly childish and perfectly fetching face. "We had a tiff. Jack and I. The usual marriage thing. I just went for a little walk. Needed air."

"Did you see anything else?"

"Anything else?"

I nodded to the two-lane asphalt road about a long city block from the gazebo. "You didn't see a car or anybody on the road over there?"

"No, I'm afraid not."

For some reason—professional nosiness, probably—I wanted to ask her what she and her husband, Jack, had been arguing about.

"I need to call Cliffie. And you need to make sure that nobody leaves. Tell them what happened and tell them that they have to stay here at least until Cliffie gets a chance to take down their names."

"My God," she said, "I can't believe it."

"What?"

"I'm actually going to let Cliffie Sykes set foot in my home."

After she left, I spent five minutes looking over the grass that stretched to the road. And found nothing. Then I went to the road itself. The other side of the asphalt was farmland, soybeans. I didn't find any notable tire tracks on either the roadside or the two-laner. I assumed that the girl had been killed elsewhere and then carried from a car parked on this road. Somebody had gone to a lot of trouble.

Everybody drifted into the front yard. About half brought their drinks. A woman cried; a man said that it was about time somebody dealt with the crime wave we were having in town. I wasn't sure what crime wave he was talking about. A Shell station had been broken into last night. Maybe that's what he had in mind.

There are three things you should know right away about Clifford Sykes Jr., the first being that when his family of rednecks came up here from the Ozarks a few generations ago, they lived not in the Knolls, which was sort of the official slums where I grew up, but on a sandy bend of the river where they bred babies, filth, and stupidity. Cliffie's grandfather tried to bring the Klan up here and even managed to burn a cross in a field until several of the men in town, including my dad, went out there with shotguns and ball bats and persuaded all the fat drunks hiding in sheets that the Klan was not wanted in these parts.

The second thing you need to know about Cliffie is that he hates me because I work for Judge Esme Anne Whitney, whose folks came out here with a lot of Eastern money in the previous century and pretty much built the town. It was almost never mentioned that this branch of the Whitney family had to leave New England rather suddenly when several major papers mentioned a major bank fraud case being brought against the Whitneys' most infamous black sheep, Esme's father.

The Whitneys ran the town until World War II came along. Esme was sent back east to school when she was seven, graduated from Smith, lived for a time in Europe, finally returned to town here with a law degree and a yen for the judicial bench, which she got with more than a little help from a Dixiecrat holdout in Harry Truman's Justice Department.

Cliffie Senior, through a series of coincidences and outright miracles, had been able to parlay his shabby little construction company into a firm that helped the army build training camps and airstrips throughout the Midwest. With his new fortune in hand, Cliffie Senior ran for mayor, won by making all sorts of foolish promises that he actually made good on, and proceeded to buy off every important person loyal to the judge's camp. All that was left to this branch of the Whitney family, in the person of Esme Anne herself, was her judgeship, several million dollars, and a dire need to fly to New York whenever she could put together a three-day vacation. Don't ever let her start telling you stories about her "brunches" with the likes of "Lenny Bernstein" and "Dick Nixon" and the various fashion designers who make her stylish clothes. Her stories of the famous are as long-winded and pretentious as a novel by Thomas Wolfe.

The town now belonged to the Cliffies, Senior and Junior, respectively.

The third thing about Cliffie is that he secretly thinks he's Glenn Ford. Back when we were in grade school together, everything was Glenn Ford Glenn Ford Glenn Ford. In the early fifties, when Ford started making a lot of Westerns, he sometimes wore a khaki outfit and carried his gun slung low. Hence, you will notice that Cliffie, as he makes his appearance here, is also dressed in khaki with his gun slung low.

I admit to a bit of hypocrisy, complaining about Cliffie walking around pretending he's Glenn; I walk around pretending I'm Robert Ryan.

I was in the driveway when Cliffie swept up in his cruiser, a hopped-up Mercury with a whip antenna that could amputate low-hanging branches if given half a chance. The ambulance was already here, along with Doc Novotony's shiny black Corvette. Doc is the medical examiner and a distant relative of Cliffie's. He's one of the few Sykes menfolk who doesn't blow his nose on his shirt sleeve.

Usually, Cliffie swaggers. And sneers. The thing is, though he had his gun and his white Stetson and his cowboy boots, he had one more thing tonight, too. His feelings of inferiority.

Most people don't ever forget being poor. As much as poverty deprives the belly, it also deprives the spirit. A big house like this, a dozen locally prominent people standing on the Jay Gatsby lawn, a hint of art and culture glimpsed through the wide front windows . . . this wasn't Cliffie territory and never would be. No matter how mean, rich, or powerful Cliffie got, he would never be accepted by people like these and he knew it.

I would have felt sorry for the dumb bastard but he would've scowled if I'd mentioned that I knew how he was feeling.

He came up and said, "Looks like these fancy friends of yours got some trouble on their hands."

"Looks like."

"One of 'em needs a lawyer, Counselor, I'll bet it won't be you. It'll be some blue-suit prick from Cedar Rapids."

"Probably."

He looked at me as if my face had broken out. "You not feeling well tonight, Counselor?"

"Why?"

He checked his wristwatch.

"Been here nearly two minutes and you haven't insulted me yet."

"That's because you and I have one thing in common tonight. We don't belong here. And we both know it. It's sort of intimidating for a couple of hayseeds from the Knolls."

He spat a stream of chewing tobacco. He usually spat in the direction of one of my shoes. The way the bad guy in the bad Westerns always shoots at the ground and makes the pitiful old drunk dance.

"Shit, Counselor, I'll bet my old man has three times as much money as Coyle here."

"I'll bet he does, too," I said. He knew damned well what I was talking about. And I knew damned well he wouldn't admit it.

Two of his men took care of business. They'd been taking police training at the state academy. They had a pretty decent knowledge of inspecting crime scenes and interviewing witnesses and identifying suspects. He looked at them now and snorted. "Those two men, they get a little bit of police school and they think they're hot shit."

"Maybe you should get a little of that training yourself. Couldn't hurt."

He gaped at me again. "What the hell's with you tonight, Counselor? You sound like one of those psychologist guys on the tube." Then, "And you tell that judge of yours not to get you involved in this one, McCain, you get me? I'd hate to have to make a fool of her again."

I almost said something but stopped myself in time. The standing battle between Judge Whitney and Cliffie took the form of her always disproving the guilt of the person Cliffie had charged with a capital crime. By this time the score was something like 37 to 0, due in no small part to the fact that Cliffie didn't know anything about investigative techniques. He always claimed he went on "hunches." Ah, those good old hunches.

Cliffie said, "Now I gotta go call the Griffins and tell them what happened. I'll just patch in through my two-way."

"Sort of the personal touch, huh, Chief?"

"You want to call them for me, Counselor? You think you'd like to make a call like that?"

He went away and came back within a few minutes. I spent the time talking to one of his deputies, who actually sounded intelligent. For a minute or so I was alone. I took in the summer moon-drift sky and the scent of grass and flowers from the nearby garden. It was a night to be twelve again, catch fireflies, and read comic books under the covers with a flashlight and dream of the girl you hope to walk home from school with some lucky day.

Cliffie said, "Well, well, Counselor, looks like you and me may be buttin' heads on this dead girl after all."

"How would that be?"

"One of my least favorite people sounds like he's in a lot of trouble."

"How does that affect me?"

"He's one of your clients. One of those punks we're always haulin' in and you're always bailin' out. Mrs. Griffin told me that her daughter and him had a terrible argument just this afternoon and that he slapped her."

I knew the name he was going to say. And I dreaded hearing it. A lot of people had predicted that he would kill somebody someday. Maybe that day had come around at last.

"David Egan, Counselor." Cliffie smirked. "He *is* a client of yours, isn't he?"

THREE

OVER THE NEXT HALF hour, I got curious about why Cliffie was spending so much time talking to Linda Dennehy. She was pretty, maybe that was why. But after the third time he walked over to his men and then came right back to Linda, I wondered what was going on.

I stood on the lawn with everybody else. As soon as Cliffie's men finished with them, the guests left. They all looked tired. They'd talked it all out for now; tomorrow, over breakfast coffee, they'd start talking about it again. And for days after that.

Linda drifted over after a time. "You about ready for that car ride, Sam?"

"Been ready."

"I think Cliffie's done questioning me."

"What was that all about?"

"The party—I came with Jane Daly. I'd left my purse in her car and needed to get it. He wanted to know if I saw anything or anybody. I didn't. Cliffie seems to think I'm hiding something because I'm afraid to be a witness. No matter how many times I told him otherwise, he'd keep coming back and telling me how he'd protect me and I shouldn't be afraid to tell him who I saw in the garage. He really thinks I saw the killer."

"That's our Cliffie. He never lets reality get in his way."

"I almost feel guilty for not having seen the killer, you know?"

"You did what you could. You told him the truth. From now on it's his problem."

I was just about to ask if she wanted to go when Cliffie appeared.

"Counselor, you could do me and this town a favor by convincing your frightened little friend that she should tell me everything she knows."

"She's told you everything she knows."

He smirked. "I see she's already told you I've been asking her for the truth."

"You want her to make up something? Maybe draw a name out of a hat?"

He looked at her and said, "You ever gone out with this David Egan, Linda?"

"I don't usually date high school boys."

"This day and age, anything's possible."

"Well, I've never dated him, Chief. I'm not sure I've ever even spoken to him."

"Pretty gal like you, maybe he's spoken to you."

"I'm afraid not."

Cliffie started to ask another question but I interrupted him. "She's told you what she knows. She's willing to sign a statement to the effect that everything's she's told you is the truth. How's that?"

"You her lawyer now, are you, Counselor?"

"I am if she needs one. Does she need one, Chief?"

He sighed. "Maybe you can make her understand, Counselor." We were talking man to man now. Girls excluded. It was as if

Linda had vanished. "Maybe you can explain how police protection works. Everywhere she goes, she'll have one of my men trailing her. And every time she's at home, I'll have a man parked nearby. I won't let anybody touch her."

Linda smiled. "That sounds very nice, Chief. Having protection like that. Unfortunately, I really don't know who the killer is."

"That's just about all she has to say, Chief. Now, we'd like to get out of here if possible."

He leaned in my direction and said, "You know these people pretty good, do you, Counselor?"

"If you mean the Coyles, I'm a friend of Jean's."

He leaned in and whispered. "Glad you're not a friend of her husband's. There's a jackass for you."

I didn't say anything.

"You come out here often?"

"A few times a year. To parties."

"I'm surprised they'd invite somebody who grew up in the Knolls out here."

"They're well-off. But that doesn't mean they're snobs."

"I'm also told that the dead girl was going out with David."

"I have to take your word for all this. I don't know anything about David's personal life. Not much, anyway. I've represented him on a few traffic charges is all."

"The way he drag races, he's gonna get himself killed one of these days. And he's gonna kill somebody else, too, while he's at it."

"I agree. And I've told him that many times."

The smile. "Well, Counselor, it was bound to happen. We had to agree with each other someday and it finally happened." Then, to Linda, "Don't leave the county without my permission."

"Darn, Linda," I said, "there goes your trip to Antarctica."

"Gosh, and I was hoping to bring back all that whale blubber, too."

"You two should go on *Ed Sullivan*," Cliffie said. "You're getting your act down real good."

"Can he do that? Order me to stay in the county?" Linda asked as Cliffie walked away. He was now a whole lot less intimidated by the house and its guests. His swagger was back. And that was the natural order of things. Cliffie was an incompetent jerk. My momentary madness of feeling sorry for him had passed.

"Of course not."

"That ride really sounds good, Sam."

"Yeah," I said, sliding my arm around her slender shoulders, "it sure does."

I always try to picture the land as it was before even the Indians arrived. Impenetrable timber and man-tall grass and prairies and meadows and hills raw with deep true colors. Enough buffalo and bison to make the ground rumble when they approached. Enough steep red limestone cliffs to provide a facsimile of life as the original cliff dwellings must have looked like. And the rushing, bank-overflowing rivers, fast and blue and slapping with fish.

At night come the mysteries that must have given even the Vikings pause, those sounds and shadows, that harsh and brazen moon, the tumbled dark ravines and the caves with their seared white bones of unknown animals—night is best of all.

We didn't talk.

You can do that sometimes after sharing a proximity to death. A car accident, all mangled metal and terrible lurid blood on the highway; or sobbing, plump swimsuited adults telling you about a five-year-old who has just drowned in the public pool; or a crowd of drunks in a parking lot where one drunken battler accidentally killed another with an unlucky punch.

There's either a lot of talk or not much talk at all.

A teenage girl had died tonight and there was nothing to say and so we said it.

There was just the wind and the smooth V-8 of the red ragtop in the moon-silver countryside: the sandpits where we'd drunk underage beer in high school; the drive-in theater that would close with the first frost but for now showed a screenful of images of rock and roll and sex and despair and death, city images out here in the country dancing on a piece of cloth; and the baseball park where the Little Leaguers dreamed of big league glory, not understanding that the cost of such glory would be their innocence.

We got KOMA on the radio, best rock-and-roll station in the country, pure rock all the way across the land from Oklahoma City, the favorite of small-town Midwestern kids and adult-kids everywhere.

I decided to talk. "I'll be your lawyer."

She didn't respond at first. Her eyes behind her glasses looked far, far away. She was pulled up on the seat with her fine legs beneath her and her hair caught in the wind.

"Will I need one?"

"Probably. Cliffie'll pester the hell out of you."

"He can't make me say anything I don't want to say."

"He can try."

"He's such an idiot."

"You can be an idiot when your old man runs the town," I said.

"That's why I like Iowa City so much better. You have a lot more privacy. And they wouldn't put up with Cliffie for thirty seconds. And it's a lot more sophisticated. I see a lot of foreign movies there. I never thought I could get used to the subtitles but I have."

I sensed she was going to tell me whatever she'd hinted at back on the patio. But she was going to work up to it.

She said, "You know he left me."

"I heard that, yes. I'm sorry."

"Something happened to me and as much as I hate to say it, I guess I can't really blame him for leaving." She hesitated. "He just couldn't handle it is all."

"Sounds like you're taking all the blame for whatever happened."

"Oh, it isn't blame so much as . . . just being real about it."

Then we didn't talk for some time. I headed back to town. The river was nice this time of night, speeding down the long, narrow asphalt with the moonlight on the dark water and campfires on the far shore up near the bend. A Piper Cub glided above the birch trees.

"Did you hear that I'd been sick?" she said.

"No, I hadn't. What was wrong?"

"Oh, you know, a woman thing."

"Are you all right now?"

"Well, the doctors think everything is going well." She tried to smile but it didn't quite work and the sadness was back on her face. "And I pray a lot. I pray all the time." Then, "I don't want to—let me put it another way. I'd like to make out with you tonight, Sam. But I can't. I hope you won't get mad."

"I'll try and control that psychotic temper of mine."

She reached out and put her hand on my shoulder. "I'm having a hard time with some—things—Sam."

"I'm sorry."

"I don't feel very . . . female these days. Do you know much about breast cancer?"

And then all her comments made sense. Same thing had happened to an aunt of mine.

"A little, I guess."

"Well, I didn't feel very female after the operation. And when my husband saw me—undressed me the first time—it wasn't his fault, but I could see how repelled he was and—and I was repelled, too. Every time I'd look in the mirror. They had to take my right breast."

She didn't cry. She simply looked out at a passenger train snaking, its lighted window like the glowing skin of a rattler, across the Midwest midnight.

"Right now, Sam, I just couldn't handle making out."

FOUR

S O Y O U H A V E N O idea how it got there?"

"God, Sam, how many times do I have to tell you? I don't have any idea at all."

"And you weren't out there last night?"

"No. Not even close."

"And you can prove that?"

David Egan said, "I can prove it but I'd rather not."

I sat on the edge of my desk and lighted a Lucky. He put his hand out. I pitched him the pack.

He said, "All I've got is the habit, Sam. I'll need a match, too."

I'd been planning to go to Iowa City for the Hawkeye game that day. But not now. Not with the events of last night. I'd have to send Dad and Mom on alone.

David Egan was the local heartbreaker. Even my part-time secretary, Jamie—who was so in love with her boyfriend, Turk, that she wore two of his rings, both suitably stuffed with pink angora, one on her wedding finger, the other on a chain around her neck—her cheeks flushed, and she dithered even more than usual when Egan was around. She claimed Egan looked just like Tony Curtis—which came as news to me and, I assumed, would come as news to Tony. Egan had been raised by two maiden aunts after his drunken father rambled west and got himself killed under mysterious circumstances and his mother died young of heart disease. There were two distinct David Egans. Now that he was in trouble, he was the humble Egan. But there was a harsh side, too, the self-pitying side that always let you know how tough his life had been and implied it should be your turn to have a little of his hard luck. This only seemed to attract the girls, who foolishly thought they could use maternal skills to take away his bitterness. He was a heartbreaker and proud of it. He was also an obsessive drag racer and that was how I knew him. I'd had to represent him in court several times because his souped-up black Mercury just dragged him into trouble again and again.

"We've got two things we need to clarify before Cliffie finds you," I said to Egan.

Cliffie had gone looking for Egan last night. But Egan had gotten the word first and hidden out in the abandoned grade school. He called me around dawn. It was now nearly 9 A.M.

"I could really use some breakfast," he said, the way any seventeen-year-old kid would. And then he made a rasping sound that quickly became a wheeze. His asthma. The one flaw in the portrait of the teenage rebel as seen on drive-in screens throughout the land. The one flaw that marred the snapshot of this particular seventeen-year-old in his James Dean red nylon jacket, white T-shirt, and jeans was the fact that he was about to be charged with murder.

He fought his asthma a few minutes.

"I could use some breakfast myself, David. But right now we'll have to make do with this really shitty coffee I made. Then we're going over to Cliffie's and you're going to turn yourself in."

"You sure about this, McCain?"

"Positive. But now I want to know about Sara Griffin."

He shrugged. "Then I'll need another cigarette."

I tossed the pack back.

"First of all, what were you and Sara Griffin arguing about yesterday?"

"I'd rather not say."

"Then go get another lawyer."

"Hey, man, what bug crawled up *your* ass?"

"You don't help me, David, there's no way I can help you. We're just wasting each other's time."

"Shit," he said and stared down at his hands. Without looking up, he said, "All my life I've been screwed."

"No time for your self-pity, David. Answer my question. What were you arguing about last night?"

"I asked her to marry me and she said no."

Well, well. People had said crazier things to me but at the moment, I couldn't think of any. The daughter of one of the richest families in town and David Egan, seventeen-year-old high-school dropout, asks her to marry him.

"Did you slap her?"

"No. I just—I sort of brushed her. I pulled back at the last minute. I really did."

"What was your relationship with her?"

"I am—was—in love with her."

"Were you intimate?"

"You mean did I sleep with her?"

"Yes, did you sleep with her?"

"No. There was . . . somebody else."

"Who?"

He scowled. "I never knew."

I hesitated, making sure I could make myself be understood without sounding harsh. "She was beautiful and she was rich and she was seventeen. Why did you think she might say yes when you asked her to marry you?"

A smirk. "That isn't what you want to say, man. You want to say why was I dumb enough to fall in love with somebody out of my class."

"All right. If that's the way you want to put it."

He paused, stared down at his hands again. "I don't know how to say this exactly. I—she—when I was with her I felt . . . special. I didn't feel like some punk who hung around with a bunch of simps from the Knolls. I was part of her world. They have a maid, man. And three cars. And their house—hell, it's a mansion—it's so big I used to get lost walking around in it. I was somebody when I was there. I don't know how else to say it. There wasn't any other girl who made me feel that way."

"What was wrong with Rita?"

"Her old man owns some horse stable. Big deal."

"How about Molly?"

He shrugged. "Molly—she's like me. She wants to improve herself. Step up the ladder, so to speak. I think that's cool. But it doesn't help me. I need somebody who's already there. Somebody with a maid and three cars in the garage."

I walked over and got myself some more coffee. "That's number one. You were arguing because Sara rejected you. Now number two. Where were you last night?" I went back to my perch on the desk.

"I can't tell you who I was with."

"Why not?"

"Because I gave my word."

"I need to know, David. And right now."

"I can't, McCain. I really can't."

"Why wouldn't this person want to help you?"

"Because," he said, "she's married."

"Great, David," I said, "just great."

FIVE

I HAD JUST LOCKED the outside door to my office when I heard a young woman's voice say, "Oh, God, David, there you are!"

By the time I reached my ragtop, sleek, copper-haired Molly Blessing was in David's arms, sobbing joyfully into his neck.

Before meeting up with Sara Griffin, David had spent his youth going back and forth between Molly and Rita Scully. Most people found it pretty funny, the way he'd drop one and go back to the other. But a few, me among them, found it more sad than comic.

Molly Blessing was the daughter of the town's most successful barber. Her dad cuts my hair. I've known her since she was four and used to help her dad sweep up all the hair. She'd told me once that she'd been in love with David since kindergarten. Her parents had never approved. David wasn't exactly what middle-class parents wanted in the way of son-in-law material.

Molly's rival, Rita, came from the Knolls, was pretty in a striking jet-haired, green-eyed way, but was neither as refined nor as subtle as Molly. When she and David battled, which was frequently, they often battled with fists. Rita once gave him a black eye, which was an accomplishment for a girl who barely cleared five-one and one hundred pounds.

If there was a pattern in all the breakups and make-ups, I couldn't find it. David would be with one of them for two or three months and then go back to the other. Then he'd start running around, grabbing every girl he could. Then he'd go back to either Molly or Rita. It had to be a rough way to live.

None of this inspired a great relationship between the two girls. Their own battles were frequent and clamorous enough to feed the gossip machine for weeks at a time. They'd never gotten into a fist fight—Molly was as delicate as a long-stemmed glass— but other than that it was no holds barred. Windshield smashed. Tires stabbed flat. Insults. Threats. Dirty names on telephone booths and building walls all over town. Molly's father once got a restraining order against Rita. And Rita's father threatened to punch out Molly's father if his daughter ever again wrote "Slut!" on the family's 1951 Hudson, a bathtub-shaped vehicle that needed no help in disgracing itself.

And on and on, each girl as creatively petty as her rival—the grief, humiliation, rage extending from grade school all the way through high school graduation this past summer.

Molly wore a brown sweater and a short brown-and-yellow-checked skirt. The brown kneesocks and penny loafers completed the preppie look. For all her looks, though, there had always been a sense of the frantic about Molly, as if she expected her world to come apart at any moment. I liked her; I liked both Molly and Rita, actually, different as they were. Both of them were good for David.

"Where are you going?" Molly asked when her arms slid away from David.

"McCain's taking me to the police station."

She grabbed my arm. "Oh, no, Mr. McCain. Don't you know what Cliffie'll do to him?"

"I know what Cliffie'll try to do to him, Molly. But I won't let him."

"Please, don't make him go there, Mr. McCain."

I took her hand. It was slender but soft, not unlike Molly herself. "Look, Molly, Cliffie has good reason to talk to David. And it'll only look worse for David if he keeps trying to avoid it. Cliffie could've put out an arrest warrant if he'd wanted to, but I convinced him to let me try and find David. David called me, which is a point in his favor, and which I'll really play up with Cliffie. And I'll also play up that David came in of his own volition. That will help, too."

"Oh, David," she said, leaning against him, sliding her arm around him. I imagined David was feeling the full force of her love and it had to move him. Very few of us get that kind of love in our lifetimes.

"We'd better go," I said gently as possible.

We got in the car. Molly hung on David's door like a camp follower unwilling to let go of her soldier.

"Will you call me as soon as you finish with Cliffie?" she said.

"I can imagine how your folks are taking this."

"To hell with my folks," Molly said, sounding harder and tougher than I'd ever heard her. I was impressed. She said to me, quietly, "I know who killed Sara, Mr. McCain."

"You do?"

"Rita killed her. She despised Sara. She dumped manure in the back seat of Sara's VW."

"I'll keep that in mind."

I backed away from her, feeling guilty as hell. She looked lost, waving a feeble, lonely good-bye.

The downtown area was pretty bare for a warm Saturday

afternoon. All the trees were doing their fire dances, the air was autumn-melancholy, and the town park was empty except for a young couple who looked enviably in love. He was sort of feeling her up but with some dignity, if you know what I mean.

I pulled in next to two patrol cars and a couple of private cars. In the back of the police station I saw Cliffie arguing with Rita Scully.

Cliffie didn't see us until we were only a few feet away. Rita didn't see us because her back was to us. She was shaking her fist in Cliffie's face. She looked as good from the front as the back, faded jeans and an emerald green sweater loving every bit of her small but perfect body.

"Only you would be stupid enough to believe that David would kill somebody," she shouted.

"Things happen like that all the time."

"And why would he drag her out to the Coyles? That doesn't make any sense, either."

"Well, look who's here," Cliffie said, smirking.

When she turned and saw David, Rita did exactly what Molly had done. She hurried to him and threw her arms around his neck. Then she kissed him with great open passion.

"He better save up all that good lovin'," Cliffie said. "He ain't gonna be gettin' much of it in prison. Least not the kind he wants, anyway."

"He's not going to prison."

"Counselor, there's one thing I admire about you."

"Only one?"

"Your faith in your own legal abilities. You're about as unsuccessful a lawyer as this town has ever seen but you're always makin' these grand claims about how you're gonna save this one and that one from prison."

Once again, I refrained from reminding Cliffie how often he'd lost to Judge Whitney and me. I was willing to hurt his feelings; that wasn't it. But his ego would be hurt and he'd be snake-mean to deal with if I reminded him of what a rube he was.

Rita went Molly one better. She started sobbing and she wouldn't let go of David. You could see how embarrassed he was. But you could also see how aggrieved she was. She had to stand on tiptoes to hold him around the neck. She looked as childlike now as Molly had disappearing in my rearview mirror.

Cliffie said, "All right, Egan. Let's go inside. Say good-bye to the pretty lady."

I said, "I want to go along."

"I'll call you when you're needed, Counselor. First, I want to fingerprint him and get a couple of beauty pictures. We'll make sure not to ask him anything till you're with him." He laughed. "He's had a lot of time to work up an alibi. I'll bet it's a doozy."

The alibi was what I was worried about. Married or not, the woman needed to come forward.

David came over. "I'm ready."

"Just be sure not to tell the counselor here that we worked you over with a rubber hose."

"Is he always this funny?" David asked me.

"This is the good stuff. Wait till you hear the bad stuff."

"Two funny guys," Cliffie said. "Two very funny guys."

Rita drifted over. She apparently didn't want to get anywhere near Cliffie. Given her temper, she might have attacked him.

"You have a hankie, Mr. McCain?"

"Sure."

She put the hankie to her pert, freckled nose. She had one of those faces doubly pretty because of its vitality.

"He didn't kill her," she said.

"I know."

"But that damned Cliffie'll railroad him."

"We won't let him."

She looked at me. "Who'll pay you, Mr. McCain?"

"We'll work it out."

She glanced around the gravel parking lot. The cruisers. The Jeep. Then she looked at the two-story concrete block building. The bars on the windows. The bars never really get to you until you know somebody behind them.

"Will they hurt him?"

"No."

"Cliffie hurt you that time."

Couple years back Cliffie, half drunk, had a good time jabbing me with his nightstick. Hard enough to inflict real pain and draw real blood. I'd brought an excessive force suit against him, then agreed to drop it if he went on the local radio station and apologized to me. He did it. He made a joke of it in places. And he hinted that he'd been justified in doing it. But he did it and that was enough for me.

"Things have changed. The courts are a lot tougher on cops these days."

"Even with Cliffie's old man running the town?"

I nodded. "Even with that."

"You want to know who killed her?"

"Who?"

"Molly. Molly Blessing."

"Why would Molly kill her?"

"Because she was so jealous of Sara Griffin."

"And you weren't?"

"I don't have the temper Molly does."

I smiled. "C'mon, Rita."

"No, really. Everybody thinks because she's so quiet and everything, she doesn't blow up like I do. But she came at me with a knife one night. I thought she was going to kill me."

"Funny, Molly said the same thing about you."

"That I tried to stab her?"

"No, that you killed Sara."

"That bitch."

I nodded to the door. "I think I'll go inside. Maybe I don't trust Cliffie as much as I said."

"That bitch really said I killed Sara?"

I gave her shoulder a little squeeze. "That's what she said, Rita."

"Bitch."

"Yeah, I think you said that already."

SIX

MOM AND DAD GOT the Hawkeye tickets, which was
fine because their wedding anniversary was coming up and
Mom had never been to a college football game before and was a
lot more excited about going than I would have suspected. I told
them that Mrs. Goldman would let them into my apartment and
where they'd find the tickets.

"I forgot to bring her that chocolate-chip cookie recipe," Mom
said on the phone. "The one with the coconut in it. I'd better be
sure and dig it out this time."

The interrogation consisted of Cliffie controlling his natural
instincts because I was there and David not saying much except,
"I didn't kill her."

"If you didn't kill her, then who did?"

"I think," I said, "that's sort of your job, isn't it?"

"You stay out of this, McCain. He did it and you know he did
it and I know he did it and he knows he did it. And I'm gonna to
stay here until he admits it."

Or at least until the Hawkeyes scored. "Shit," Cliffie said, "I
wanted to listen to the game. Have somebody bring in a radio."

I don't know about you but I want my villains to be arch villains. Fu Manchu, now there was a villain. Same for Batman's nemesis, The Joker, and all the various nemeses Tarzan of the Apes ran up against. Villains through and through.

You see all the great crime movies and the crooked, stupid cops in them are tireless in their villainy. Eye gouging? Brass knuckles? Shin kicking? And that's just for starters. But Cliffie was sort of a villain but not sort of a villain, too. He would suddenly lunge at David and shout in his face, "You killed her, you little punk! Now just admit it!" And then before David could say even a word—assuming, of course, that he wanted to say a word—Cliffie would say to his patrolman, "Turn that radio up a little, will ya?"

I'm pretty sure Fu Manchu never listened to a football game while he was interrogating somebody. Sort of spoils the effect, wouldn't you say?

I was in the middle of repeating my 842 best reasons for letting David go when Cliffie jumped up in the air like the world's oldest male cheerleader. His holster flapped against his leg. His badge jumped on his chest. His face got a deep, beery red. "Touchdown!" he cried, slamming his fist into his palm. "Kill those bastards! Kill those bastards!"

I hoped that wasn't the cheer going through the stands. I wouldn't have wanted my Mom's first Hawkeye game to be spoiled by an obscene cheer. (I could hear her now: "I never knew they used language like that at those football games, Sam. I was sort of surprised.")

The score was tied at halftime and Cliffie had to make a decision. He said, "He's guilty."

"Yes, I know you think he's guilty. But that doesn't make him guilty." Then I said, "I'd like to talk to you in the hall."

"Why?"

"Just because it's sort of personal."

"You're wasting your time, trying all those legal tricks on me."

"Two minutes is all I need."

He looked at his officer, the narrow one leaning against the wall with his arms folded across his chest. "Can you believe the shit this guy asks me to do?" Cliffie asked him.

The officer grinned around his toothpick. "He's a ballsy bastard."

"Hear that, McCain? 'A ballsy bastard.' That about says it all."

"Yeah, I heard. Now could I have two minutes of your time in the hall?"

So we went into the hall.

He said, "I'm not gonna let him go."

"I didn't want to resort to this but I don't have any choice."

I couldn't believe he didn't know what was coming but it was obvious he didn't.

"I want to remind you about the last three murder cases we've had in this town."

And then he knew what was coming. And I almost felt sorry for him.

"You arrested three people right off the bat for each murder."

"I had good reason to."

"Maybe. But each person turned out to be innocent."

His cheeks were tinted a faint red now. He was not happy to be reminded of his past limitations as an investigator.

"They talk about that, Chief."

"Talk about what?"

"How you've gone three for three."

"Who talks about it?"

"People. In town here."

"Bastards. I was just doin' my job."

"I'm sure I can talk Judge Whitney into approving bail."

"Hell, yes, you can. She'd do anything to embarrass me."

"This'll keep you from embarrassment, Chief. You'll name him as a suspect but you'll allow him to be bailed out. This'll make you look a lot better than locking him up for six or seven days and then finding out he's innocent."

He scowled at me. "I just noticed somethin'."

"What?"

"You never called me 'Chief' before. Now you're callin' me that all the time."

"It's a term of respect. We've had our differences personally but I still respect the office."

"You sure can sling the shit, McCain."

I grinned. "Just about as well as you."

He almost smiled. Almost. But then he caught himself, jammed a cigarette into his mouth and opened the door of the interrogation room. I followed him back in.

He stood next to David Egan.

"What if I let him go and he kills somebody else?" he said.

I looked down at David. "If he lets you go, are you going to kill anybody?"

"No," David said. He smiled.

"There you have it," I said. "His sacred word."

"Game starts again in six minutes, Chief," his patrolman said.

"People think I have such an easy job," Cliffie said to no one in particular. "Sit around and polish your badge and count your bullets and beat up a few deadbeats just for kicks. It might've been like that in the old days but it sure ain't anymore. These days a chief of police can't even find the time to squeeze in a Hawkeye game on a Saturday afternoon." He sneered at me. "Go ahead, McCain. Get him out of here. I want a fifty-thousand-dollar bond on him. But if he kills anybody else, I'm really gonna be pissed."

"And I wouldn't blame you," I said. "You shouldn't be allowed to kill more than one person a week in this town. And this kid's had his quota. That is, according to you."

"Just get the hell out of here."

On the way back to my office, I said to David, "You need to tell me who you were with last night."

"I wish I could. This is really getting serious, isn't it?"

"Yeah," I said. "Very serious."

I called Judge Whitney. She was more than happy to grant bail and to put up the money herself. "Now," she said, "you've got to find the real killer and humiliate Cliffie like you've never humiliated him before. You understand?"

Jack Coyle said, "Our girls want to move." He tried to smile. "They think our house is cursed now."

You could hear his twins playing basketball on a hoop near the garage. I'd watched them as I'd pulled up. They were as pretty as their mother but not anywhere near as delicate. They knew a lot of basketball's most hallowed dirty tricks. Especially stuff to use when the other girl was going in for a layup.

"They saw a show like that on TV once," Jean Coyle said. "Where the murdered person came back to haunt the people who lived there."

"Damned TV," Jack said. "I wish it had never been invented."

"Except for sports, of course," Jean joked.

"Yes," Jack laughed. "Except for sports."

We sat in deep leather armchairs on a screened-in porch that ran the considerable length of the north side of the house. Like the rest of the house, the porch had been created with imagination and care, the leather couch and chairs complementing the pioneer artifacts placed perfectly around the tiled floor. The Shaker settee, the coffee grinder, the oaken icebox, the framed, faded photographs of Coyle ancestors let you escape the press of the present. And that was nice every once in a while.

"I imagine you're doing battle with Cliffie," Jean said to me.

"He's letting David Egan out on bail."

"Now there's a surprise," Jack said. "I didn't think Cliffie believed in bail."

"I just made the point that everybody he'd arrested for murder over the last few years was ultimately proven innocent."

"I'm sure he liked that," Jack said. Then, the small talk portion of my visit over, he said, "So once again young Sam McCain, Boy Detective, leaps into the fray."

His remark came out just harshly enough—there was more than a hint of condescension in it—that Jean shot him a surprised look when he said it.

But Jack didn't back down. "This is going to be uncomfortable."

"Jack," Jean said. "What are you talking about? Sam was nice enough to stop out here to see how we were doing."

Amazing how quickly the air in a room can shift from placid to tense.

"Sam came out here to question us, dear. A dead girl was found in our gazebo. Sam has a client whose name he wants to clear. And in order to do that he has to find somebody else to blame for the murder. The logical place to start is the place where the body is found. In fact, I can tell you what his first two questions will be. Did our twins know Sara Griffin at all? And did either you or I know her except in passing. That's about right, isn't it, Sam?"

He'd taken over the room. He'd asked my questions for me. He was in complete control. He was as good on his screened-in porch as he was in court. He sat there in his blue turtleneck with his carefully brushed graying hair, watching to see how I'd react to the clever way he'd undermined my visit.

"Is that true, Sam? You might think we're involved in some way?" Jean sounded hurt. The beginnings of anger started deep in her lovely blue eyes. We were friends. Friends didn't come out on a lazy football afternoon and play at an inquisition.

Jack smiled with a good deal of calculated malice. "Yes, Sam, why don't you explain exactly why you're here—if what I said isn't true."

"It's just good investigative technique," I said to Jean, "to talk to everybody involved."

"We're not involved, Sam. And I resent you implying that we are. I thought you were our friend."

"God, Jean," I said. "Please don't think—"

"Sam McCain, Boy Detective," Jack said again. The smile was smug this time. He'd managed to deny me any possibility of learning anything. And he'd probably caused permanent damage between me and Jean. He'd done a good day's work and he'd done it in less than five minutes.

She stood up, magazine-ad perfect in her tan sweater and trim brown slacks. "We have a dinner party to go to tonight, Sam. You can finish your conversation with Jack."

I didn't say anything. There was nothing to say. A little more groveling wouldn't get me anything.

"You've got balls, Sam, I'll give you that," Jack said after his wife left.

"That's what Cliffie told me."

"Before you start feeling sorry for yourself and thinking that I low-balled you just now, put yourself in Jean's place. She goes out and finds a body in our gazebo. She'll remember that the rest of her life. Jean is a fairly sheltered person. There was nothing in her life to prepare her for something like this. The only dead person she's ever seen was her father. And that was after the mortician got him all gussied up for public display. So here you come, less than twenty-four hours after this terrible event, and you want to ask us questions about the dead girl."

"I wasn't implying a damned thing and you know it."

"No, I don't know it, Sam. You took your criminology courses at the university, you're up on modern police techniques, and you've had some luck as a private investigator. No, check that. That's condescending. Luck wasn't involved, or not much of it, anyway. So when you come out here and want to question us, how are we supposed to feel?"

"You'd do the same thing, Jack, and you know it."

That was the first thing I'd said that seemed to impress him. He looked at me a long moment and said, "I suppose I would." Then, "You went all the way through school with her, Sam. You were always one of her favorites. She was rich and beautiful and she didn't care a tinker's damn that you came from the Knolls. She's always loved you—and I mean that, loved you—and here you come all of a sudden, altering your entire relationship by asking her and her husband some pretty pointed questions."

"How do you know they were pointed? I didn't even get to ask them."

"C'mon, Sam. Don't try and shit a shitter. We're both defense lawyers. We know how it all works and what it all means."

I leaned back in my comfortable leather armchair, drained the last of the Pepsi in the tall glass with the little pink terrycloth cover on it, and said, "So did either of you know her well, Jack?"

He stood up. He was so tall he looked like a totem pole, an upper-class totem pole. He said, "I admire you for asking it, Sam. That's what you want in a lawyer and an investigator." He put a hard hand on my shoulder and began to pull me up. "Now, I hope you'll admire me for defending the sanctity of my home and asking you to leave."

He was still very much in control.

SEVEN

"YOU MEAN YOU DIDN'T go to the Hawkeye game?"

"I'm not much of a sports fan, Sam. Never was, actually."

"You could get deported to Missouri for saying that."

Hesitation. "I'm sorry about last night."

I was in jeans and a sweatshirt and a beer, sitting in my apartment with my feet on the coffee table and thinking about how stupid-looking toes are.

"Sorry? For what?"

"Oh, you know. Telling you about—everything."

"I had a very nice time last night."

"I'm kind of screwed up now."

"I've been kinda screwed up my whole life. Not to pull rank on you, you understand."

She laughed. "I had a good time, too, but I don't think it was fair to you. You know, you should have certain expectations and all."

"You let me worry about my expectations. Really, Linda, I want to see you again."

"Sam, it's just—it's not a good time."

"You could make it a good time."

"You really think so?"

"Sure. We could go have some dinner someplace and then just go for a ride the way we did last night."

"But—what happens when the night's over?"

"I come home and take a cold shower and sit in an ice bath and read the Bible. Same thing I do every night."

Her laugh again. It was a small, shy, affecting laugh. "You clown."

"You know you want to go."

"And how do you know that?"

"I can just tell. I have these powers."

"It'll get awful frustrating for both of us at some point."

"We'll worry about that when we get to that point. How's that?"

"I really appreciate this, Sam."

"What the hell are you talking about? Listen, and I'm being serious now. I'm not doing you a favor. This isn't some kind of pity date. I like you. Last night I had a good time—if you discount the underlying existential dread that's always with me, I mean."

This time she giggled. "I think that's what I have. Existential dread. And that sounds a lot more impressive than telling people you're depressed. Just about everybody's depressed. But not all that many people have existential dread. I'm not even sure what it means and I'm impressed."

"Maybe we'll fall in love."

"Oh, Sam, c'mon."

"Why not? You're lonely and I'm lonely and you're short and I'm short."

"And you have existential dread and I have existential dread."

"See, what did I tell you? Sounds like love to me."

"So what time are you planning on picking me up?"

"How about seven?"

"I'm staying here at my mom's. Not in Iowa City."

"I'm looking forward to it."

"So am I."

"Oh," she said. "I almost forgot. I was working in the emergency ward one night about six months ago. I had to substitute because there was a very bad virus going around and a lot of staff were home sick. Anyway, this woman came in. She'd cut her wrists. She was in pretty bad shape. We got her fixed up and then she took off. You're probably wondering what the point of this is."

"I'm getting a little curious."

"The woman was Brenda Carlyle."

"Mike Carlyle's wife?" Mike Carlyle being the owner of the most successful local lumberyard, and a former All–Big Ten running back.

"Right."

"Was Mike with her?"

"No. That's what was so funny about it. David Egan brought her in. I walked in on them once and he was kissing her."

EIGHT

THE GRIFFINS LIVED IN one of those venerable old brick mansions that had probably looked venerable and old the day the builders finished it. It belonged in one of those sappy MGM British romances with Greer Garson, all noble and cold, and Ronald Coleman, all noble and hesitant. They'd each do three or four noble things in the tedious course of the flick and then one of them would die doing something so noble it was difficult to even speak about it. Personally, I prefer *Hot Rods from Hell*.

There were vines up the ass (and on all sides of the house, too) and mullioned windows that bespoke even greater antiquity than the vines. A blue Caddy convertible and a dark green Caddy sedan were in their proper garage slots. The doors were open for some reason. The drive and a half block in either direction were jammed with new and expensive cars of various kinds.

Inside, amid all their friends consoling the Griffins, there would be canapés and sandwiches and hard liquor served by a maid who made less in a lifetime than most of the men present made in a year and who probably worked twice as hard. It was my class anger and sometimes it was fine, resenting the upper class, and sometimes it wasn't fine, not when one of their daughters had been killed and I was petty enough to deprive them of my pity.

I would have made a good Marxist if only I could have believed in all the economic and sociological horseshit the Commies hand out.

I said a kind of prayer for the soul of poor Sara Griffin and also a kind of prayer for her parents. My older brother had died. None of us in the family, even all these years later, was ever again quite the same. The Griffins, despite the two fine and shiny cars in their open garage, would never again be quite the same, either.

No way I was going to go inside and try to talk to them with all the company they had.

Late afternoon now, autumn sky ripening into the color of grape and blood as a quarter-moon traced itself against the blue of the sky between gold-outlined clouds. There's a special quality to the loneliness of dusk, a melancholy more brooding even than the night's. I had always felt it as a child and felt it still.

I decided to get ready. A shower and fresh clothes would knock the mood out of me. I felt ridiculously eager to see Linda again, to be bound up in that quiet, sensible, good-girl prettiness of hers, the gray gaze so eternal and wise behind her glasses. How fitting she should be a nurse, I thought. And then smiled. It didn't take much to tumble me down the rabbit hole of infatuation. And with Linda I sensed the tumble would be worth the risk.

One hour later, shaved, showered, smelling of Old Spice and Lucky Strikes, I stood at the door of her mother's two-story white frame house on a narrow working-class street that showed—with its shiny new cars and all the new home repairs—how well most people were doing in the United States at the moment. There had been some violent economic ups and downs after the war, but for the most part, this was the golden age of America. There were jobs aplenty, several years of peace following the Korean War, college money for anybody who needed it, Playboy clubs, American Bandstand, the Twist, and the Flintstones, and who the hell could ask for more than that?

She was surprised to see me. She wore a quilted robe. I could smell supper. It smelled very good. She said, "Didn't you get my—"

I handed her the note she'd thumbtacked to my back door. "I believe you left this at my place."

She looked flustered for only a moment and then said, over her shoulder, "Mom, I'll be on the porch a few minutes."

"Supper's almost ready, honey."

"I know, Mom. I'll be right in."

When the door was closed, she said, "My mom's so sweet. She really is. But I'll always be her little girl, emphasis on 'little.'"

"So how do you explain that?" I said, flicking the note she'd kept in her slender fingers.

"I was going to explain it to you in person but then when you weren't there—"

"Chickened out, huh?"

"Yeah. I'm sorry, Sam."

There was a swing on the porch. I took her hand and led her to it and we sat side by side.

"I keep trying to put it into words, Sam, and I can't. So you'll understand, I mean. I was so excited when we were riding around last night—I felt so much better than I had in two years—but then when I got home and went to bed and started thinking of things . . . I just feel foolish, Sam. That's the best way to put it, I guess. Foolish that I got married so young and foolish that I'm back living at home and foolish that I can't deal with this better. My being sick, I mean."

"You're not sick now."

"No, not physically, anyway. But mentally." She tapped her sweet Midwestern head.

I took her hand. "We're all foolish."

"Oh, Sam, you don't have to try and make me feel better. I should be doing that for myself."

"I'm not kidding. We're all foolish. Foolish with ourselves, foolish with other people. And we're too tough on ourselves about it. Life's tough and unfair and it doesn't make a whole lot of sense. So we do and say foolish things because it's all we know how to do. You're going through a very rough time—something most people won't have to face in their whole lifetime—and you're trying to adjust to it. And you're doing a whole hell of a lot better job of it than I would."

She put her head on my shoulder. I liked it. I liked it a lot. The stars had started to come out. We stayed in that position and then we started to swing. Just a little bit. But the rhythm was nice and so was the cool, clean chill on the wind.

"I'm not going to give up, Linda."

"I hope you don't."

"Tomorrow night we've got a date."

"I'd like that."

"And I don't want any notes left on my door."

"There won't be any."

"And I don't want any we-now-interrupt-this program-messages on TV to tell me the date's off, either. When I'm watching professional wrestling, I don't want some announcer cutting into the match."

She laughed softly. "None of those, either."

"And I'll expect you to wear that perfume you were wearing last night."

"I promise. I don't have any other kind of perfume, anyway."

"And one other thing."

"What's that, Sam?"

I kissed her on the mouth. I started to pull back but she held me there, slender fingers against the back of my neck.

"What I was going to say," I said finally, "was that I care about you. All of a sudden last night it just happened."

The gray gaze got impish, amused. "As I recall, you fall in love pretty easily."

"I'm not sure I'm falling in love. I don't know what it is. Except every time I think of you I feel a whole lot better than I have in quite awhile. And I get this really urgent need to see you."

She was just about to say something when the front door opened and her mom stuck her head out. I was back in eighth grade again, tense about moms, and hoping I didn't say anything stupid or unforgivable.

"Oh, hi, Sam, haven't seen you in a long time," said her mom, who looked very much like her daughter. "I didn't realize you were still here. Would you like to stay for supper?"

"Afraid I can't, Mrs. Dennehy. I just stopped by to say hi to Linda."

She smiled. "Well, say hi to your folks. I always see them at mass but that's about all these days."

"I'll be right in, Mom."

"Nice to see you again, Sam."

"Nice to see you, too, Mrs. Dennehy."

Linda walked me to the edge of the porch. "I wish it were tomorrow night."

"I could pick you up later tonight."

She took my hand and kissed me on the cheek. "No, let me live in that 'glow of expectation' they're always talking about in those romance novels I read."

"It's a deal, then. We'll both glow for the next twenty-four hours and I'll see you right here tomorrow night."

This time she kissed *me* on the mouth. Not for long. "I'd have kissed you longer but Mrs. Sullivan is peeking out her curtain from across the street."

"Want to put on a real show for her?"

She took my shoulders, turned me forward like a wooden soldier, and then set me marching off to my ragtop.

I honked at her as I pulled away. She waved good-bye with a girly hand. Don't you love it when they wave good-bye with a girly hand?

NINE

KENNY CHESMORE'S GOT ONE of those tiny silver house trailers that the military used in army camps during the war. After the fighting stopped, you could get them cheap. A lot of people did, especially GIs who went to college on the GI Bill.

Kenny's trailer was set up in the shade of a giant oak with branches of mythic proportion. Easy to imagine Arthur's knights sleeping beneath its mothering wings on a stormy night preceding the battle next day.

Or in a more modern context, a pornographer cranking out twenty pages of pure art a day.

Ladies and gentlemen, meet Kenny Chesmore. The typewriter you hear is his, a sweet little Olympia portable of a model they don't make anymore. I've offered him $150 for it. He won't take it.

Out front there's a big, lazy golden collie that butterflies like to pick on and who steadfastly refuses to go outside when the thermometer strikes below thirty. His name is Herbert.

As the door opened you could see for yourself the kind of image Kenny chooses to project for himself—beatnik. Bohemian.

Outsider. The short dark hair combed forward. The goatee. The ragged gray T-shirt. The wrinkled chinos. The dirty white tennies. I'm not sure where this "beatnik" uniform came from—I've never seen any of the holy trinity, Kerouac-Ginsberg-Corso, wearing anything like it. But all you have to do is go to a city and you'll seen dozens if not hundreds of such getups. Kenny also has a bumper sticker on his door—KHRUSCHEV IS A COMMIE. Kenny likes what they call sick jokes.

When he's not writing, he's usually in a political demonstration of some kind in Chicago, which is four hours away. I'd accompanied him to the one for Caryl Chessman and the one for civil rights but some of the others bothered me enough to stay away from. Any group that is willing to forgive Joseph Stalin for all his atrocities is not a group I want to be part of.

The inside of Kenny's trailer is, as you might imagine, a garbage dump of dirty clothes, pizza wrappers, books of every size and description, stacks of records running to some really good stuff such as Sara Vaughan and Gerry Mulligan, and a huge Admiral console TV. Kenny likes his politicians to be twenty-four inches. He thinks it makes it easier for them to hear when he screams at them about what lying capitalist devils they are. He's right, of course—I like capitalism but it sure has produced more than its share of devils—it's just that he's awfully damned noisy about it.

The windows were open so the trailer smells weren't too bad. He gets some fresh breeze off the wide creek that runs in back of his place. He also gets some interesting animals, especially the raccoons and the possums that manage to break into his trailer whenever he's gone. One day I pulled up to find him out. But there were three raccoons staring out at me from his living room window.

He has a small table on which he both writes and eats. You can tell when he's about to eat because just before he puts his TV dinner into the tiny oven, he shoves his typewriter to the far edge of the table. Dinner, as they say, is served.

On the wall, high and just to the right of the table, are six or seven of his latest paperback covers thumbtacked to the wall. He makes three hundred dollars a book and usually does one a month. The covers are usually photographs of buxom women wearing as little as the law will allow. They all say "For mature readers only" somewhere near the title. The only place you can buy them in Black River Falls is down at the Union cigar store along the river. You tell the guy what your favorite brand of literature is and he always winks at you and says, "Okay, you like them there zippy books, do ya?" He always says "zippy." He's some kind of immigrant, just nobody has ever figured out what kind. Then he stoops low, lifts up a cardboard box, and gives you time alone to look through the various titles.

The covers Kenny had on his wall now all seemed to share a certain theme.

TRYST FOR TRIPLES

THREE-WAY THRUST

THRILLS FOR THREE

He handed me a Pepsi—Kenny drinks booze even less than I do—as I said, "What happened to lesbians?"

"They're sorta out right now. Ménage à trois is in."

"Ah," I said.

"The French publishers started it."

"Ah, the French."

"Hell, in Denmark they're doing bestiality with bondage."

"Ah, the Dens."

"I wish the missionary position would come back. It's a lot easier to write. I get a headache thinking up all this stuff. I've never done a three-way, have you?"

"Several times."

I've always wanted to use the word "agape." And that's just how Kenny looked. Agape. "You have?"

"We went all night."

"No shit?"

"No shit. We would've gone longer except the one sheep got tired out."

"You asshole."

"I'm from Black River Falls, Kenny. People from Black River Falls don't have three-ways."

"I'll bet they do. They just don't talk about it." He frowned at his typewriter as if it were deeply disappointing to even gaze upon. "I gotta come up with some pages here. I've got four three-way scenes to write and the rules are each one has to be at least fifteen hundred words. That's a lot of three-wayin.'"

"Occupational hazard, I suppose." I paused, "Mind if I pick up that stale sandwich and sit on the chair?"

"Oh, yeah, I guess I haven't had much time to clean the old place up. I just got back last night."

"Where'd you go?"

"Berkeley. It's really wild out there. It's like this one big huge enclave of beats. Lots of chicks, too. No bras, either. You can see their breasts swinging under their sweaters and blouses. It's like one of my books coming true."

"You get laid?"

He shrugged. "I came close."

"Well, that's better than nothing. And you're doing better than I am."

"No nookie, huh?"

I shook my head. "I'm a virgin again."

"Don't tell anybody I went to Berkeley and didn't get laid, okay?"

"That wouldn't be good for the old reputation, I guess. Especially for a pornographer. 'He couldn't get laid even in Berkeley.' Wow, that'd be some epitaph."

"Please, McCain. I've told you, I don't write pornography."

"I'm sorry, I forgot. For a 'writer of erotica.'"

He leaned back in his writing chair and picked up his pack of Kools.

"I still don't know how you can smoke menthols," I said. "It's like lighting up a box of cough drops."

"Yeah, but as much as I smoke, I tend to get sore throats."

Two ashtrays overflowing. And a dead beer can with a cigarette filter sticking out of it. I guess I saw his point.

"I got back at six last night and went right to work. I've done seventeen thousand words. That's nearly a third of a book."

"How many orgasms you figure in seventeen thousand words?"

He smiled. "Plenty. But the only time you look me up is when you want some scuttlebutt, McCain. So let's get to it. I want to get back to work here. I'm trying to hit twenty-five thousand words in twenty-four hours. That'd be a personal record."

"You told me once you did thirty thousand words in twenty-four hours."

"Yeah, but I was lying. This would be for real."

"You really should think of running for political office, Kenny. You lie so well."

You could hear all those Kools in his sharp, scratchy laugh. I don't expect my voice sounds any better.

I said, "Brenda Carlyle."

"I'd like to see *her* breasts swinging free underneath a sweater."

"I hear David Egan has had that privilege."

"That's an old story."

Kenny had always known all the gossip in town. Even with all his traveling these days, he still knew more about the private lives of our little burg than anybody else, including the three ministers, the priest, all four beauty parlors, and Cliffie's police force combined. A lot of these stories found their way, disguised of course, into Kenny's books. He'd written me into a couple of them as a short private eye named "Bullets McGee," a name I think he stole from Raymond Chandler but I'm not sure.

"Could you elaborate a little?" I said.

Kenny took a hit from his Kool. I could taste that menthol crap even over here. "He did lawn work for her husband, Mike. It was pure D. H. Lawrence. Brenda and Mike haven't gotten along in years. She starts talking to Egan—and nobody can sling the lady bullshit like that kid—and there you go."

"Instant paperback novel."

"You bet."

"Still going on?"

"On and off. You know Egan's problem. When he's with one girl, he wants to be with another girl. I'll bet *he* could get laid if he went to Berkeley."

"I'll bet he could get laid just walking down the street."

He grinned. "I always wanted to be handsome."

"I always wanted to be tall and handsome."

"Well, I always wanted to be tall and handsome and rich. And have a schlong out to here."

I laughed. "You pretty much covered the bases." Then, "Then there's always Sara Griffin."

"Sad case."

"Man, I guess."

"They covered it up by saying she went to England on some kind of foreign exchange thing."

"Yeah," I said. "She went to the nuthouse. How'd you find out?"

He inhaled deeply of his box of burning cough drops. "This nurse I interviewed for *Nympho Nurses*. I put it in a nuthouse, figured that'd be a different angle. And that way I could put transvestites and ax murderers and people who rip out their own eyeballs all in the same novel."

"Didn't Fitzgerald do something like that right after Gatsby?"

"Very funny."

"So this nurse. . . ?"

"This nurse told me about this time this girl managed to sneak away from the nuthouse and meet her lover in this nearby motel."

"Her lover?" New information. "How old was she?"

"Let's see, Sara probably would've been fifteen, probably."

"This nurse tell you who her lover was?"

"They never found out. All they know is that it was some older man. His forties maybe. This is what they got from the motel guy, anyway."

"What happened to Sara?"

"More shock treatment. Kept her a month longer than they'd originally planned."

"Then she came back here?"

"Finished high school. And met your client David Egan. Which wasn't exactly what her folks wanted. They'd spent a lot of time and laid out a lot of jack keeping her away from this older man, and then she picks up with Egan. For her it was strictly friendship. For him, he went gaga. That's why he dropped out of high school. He was so brokenhearted over her, he couldn't concentrate. But what can you expect from somebody who came from his background? He's had a rough life."

"That's crap, Kenny," I said, more sharply than I needed to. "A lot of killers come from wealthy families and a lot of very good, hard-working, moral people come from the slums."

"Wow, sounds like you're going over to the other side. You going to that Dick Nixon rally tomorrow night? I plan to go. I hear his wife is going to wear a bikini."

"Asshole," I said. "It's just that half the criminals I represent give me the same story. They have bad lives so they want to make sure other people have bad lives, too. I get tired of it. David could at least be honest with these girls."

"Tell him, not me."

"I plan to."

I stood up.

"You reading anything good these days?" Kenny said.

"A lot of Gil Brewer." Brewer was a good Gold Medal writer, whose paperbacks with the luridly swanky covers I always buy and that seem to distress nearly everybody in town. They think I should be reading great literature—which I do, actually—even though they themselves haven't read a novel since the teacher threw them to the floor and jammed *Silas Marner* down their throats.

"Yeah, he's great. Got that melancholy down. Always about a woman. He can break your heart. One of these days I'm gonna write a Gold Medal."

"I wish you would, Kenny. You're a good writer." He was. Amid all that writhing and gasping and groaning you found some eminently sound social observation and some very nicely turned sentences in Kenny's books.

"Thanks for thinking so, McCain. But everytime I sit down to write a Gold Medal—I just freeze up. I just think I'm not good enough to pull it off."

"Just pretend you're writing your usual stuff. Your books aren't all that far from Gold Medal, anyway. Kind of sneak up on yourself."

"Yeah, the way I did when I slept with Sandy Mitchell."

"You slept with Sandy Mitchell?"

"Yeah, didn't I ever tell you?"

"You slept with the homecoming queen and you didn't tell me?"

"It's a long story."

"I'll bet."

Most guys couldn't have gotten close to Sandy Mitchell with a bag of diamonds and a submachine gun. And here was the merry pornographer sleeping with her.

"We happened to be on a picnic with some other people on that little island—Tule Island—out on the river. Anyway, they all went back in the big boat and asked if we'd take the rowboat back. It was a rental. And then this storm came. And we sort of got marooned there on the island. With all this leftover beer and stuff. And you know how it goes, we were both drunk and one thing led to another, that sort of thing. But right when it was really getting serious, I thought what if I can't do it? What if I can't perform with the homecoming queen? What am I doing with a homecoming queen? I mean, she hadn't been homecoming queen for a while—this was just a couple of years ago—and she wasn't wearing her crown or anything. But still and all, the idea of me with a homecoming queen was pretty intimidating. Here she was offering herself to me and what if I couldn't do anything? It'd be all over town. I could write all the jokes myself. He can write it but he can't do it. I just didn't have any right to be with a homecoming queen."

"I don't either."

"Exactly. You don't either. Few do, in fact, when you think about it. Very few do. Anyway, what I did was pretend she was this girl I dated the summer I worked at the fair. With the blackheads and the stuff on her teeth?"

"I always felt sorry for her," I said.

"So did I but it didn't make it any easier. Anyway, once I put her face on Sandy's face, I didn't have any trouble at all. I was batting in my own league again and everything was fine."

"And then she went and married Nick Dixon."

He smiled. "The coolest kid in high school. And if you don't believe me, just ask him."

"Yeah, excessive modesty wasn't exactly a problem he had."

"So now that's two things you're not going to tell anybody about, right, McCain?"

"Two? What else besides Berkeley?"

"That I was afraid I couldn't do it with a homecoming queen."

Sandy Mitchell. He was one lucky pornographer, he was.

TEN

I N MY HIGH SCHOOL days I always tried to have a date on Saturday nights. Tried, but usually failed. So I cruised the streets with some buddies who were every bit as hard up as I was. The bowling alley; the pizza joint; the Y, where they had mixers; all the usual places where guys went to find the girls who didn't want to have anything to do with them.

The last resort was the DX station, which the custom cars and street rods used as their home base. They only came out at night, like vampires, shined, chromed, sculpted masterpieces that even the drunkest biker—who always made clear that he thought that street rod owners were femmy—paid awe and respect. You could tell this because they didn't stove-in the street rod doors or smash in the windshield.

The custom car crowd didn't like us any more than they liked the bikers. We were just pimply kids who couldn't even get chicks on Saturday nights—the custom boys always had plenty of good-looking chicks—and so when we asked them our dopey questions, their answers were short on information and long on contempt.

But there they'd be on the drive, six or seven of the finest mechanical animals rubes like us had ever seen. And for a while it was enough in the accompanying blare of Chuck Berry and Little Richard to walk around and around these beasts and take in as much of their beauty as we could handle without fainting dead away.

The lone car on the drive tonight was David Egan's chopped and channeled black Merc. David leaned against it, cigarette hanging at an angle from the corner of his mouth, his James Dean uniform natty as always. I don't mean to imply he never changed his clothes. I was pretty sure he did. He didn't smell, anyway. But his wardrobe seemed to consist of interchangeable James Dean duds, so that even when he changed red nylon jackets, snowy white T-shirts, and jeans, his clothes looked exactly the same.

The smells of gasoline, cigarettes, and oil were pleasant on the Saturday night air as I pulled in.

Dean had taken him over completely tonight, giving me that little two-finger salute while he watched me walk toward him with squinched-up eyes. I always wondered if old folks secretly wanted to imitate Lawrence Welk.

I said, "No girl on Saturday night?"

"I could ask you the same question."

"Yeah. But I have an excuse. I'm short and stupid."

He smiled. "I don't know why you're always putting yourself down."

"I do," I said. Then, "It'd be nice if you'd write a condolence note to the Griffins."

"For what?"

In the first hours following the murder, David had been frightened enough to show only his nicest side. David the lost boy. But there was the other side, a cold and arrogant side. And I felt I was just about to hear it.

"Because she was a nice, decent, troubled kid and because some sonofabitch murdered her."

"You think I did it, don't you?"

"David, she's dead, all right? Her folks will never get over it, no matter how long they live."

"Sure they will. They're always flying off to Europe and soaking up the gin and name-dropping so much it's embarrassing. Sara couldn't stand them." He smirked. "And neither could I. But they had a nice house."

I shouldn't have done it but I did. I grabbed him by the collar of his James Dean jacket and flung him the length of his car.

"Hey, you little prick," he said.

"She's dead, David. You could at least be decent to her folks."

He straightened his jacket and T-shirt and gave me the squinted-eyes routine again.

"Just get out of here, McCain."

"She's dead, David. Her parents deserve a note of condolence."

"They'll just throw it away."

"Even if they do, it needs to be written."

The sullen face was all his own. "All the shit I've had to go through."

"That doesn't give you any right to treat women the way you do."

"They know what they're getting into."

It was a bad movie line. The desperado. The rebel no woman could tame. You could hear it coming through a tinny drive-in speaker now.

"You're taking your life out on them, David, and they deserve better. Sara and Rita and Molly are good young women."

"They hire you to say that?"

I said, "I don't want to represent you anymore, David."

He came off the car and said, "What the hell are you talking about?"

"There are other lawyers in town. I'll arrange for one of them to help you. But I'm done."

"That'll make it look like I'm guilty." Then, "You can't do this, McCain. You really can't."

"You going to write that note to the Griffins?"

"All right, God, if that's what you want me to do."

"That's a start. And knock off the heartbreaker bullshit. Everybody knows you love 'em and leave 'em, David. But you may have to face a jury here pretty soon. And you're gonna need all the friends you can get."

He smirked again. "Maybe I should wear a cassock and a Roman collar."

"It wouldn't hurt, David." I got sick of him from time to time—his childhood hadn't corrupted him but his reaction to his childhood, his self-pity, certainly had—but I hadn't ever been as sick of him as I was at this moment.

I walked away to my ragtop.

"I knew you were bluffing, McCain. I knew you wouldn't really drop me."

I said nothing. Just drove away. Leaving a bad imitation of James Dean standing alone in the muzzy yellow light of the gas station drive.

In the rearview mirror, I watched as he slipped his hands in his back pockets, pure James Dean. And now, unfortunately, pure David Egan.

ELEVEN

I'D BEEN IN MY apartment only a couple of minutes before there was a knock on the inside door. Mrs. Goldman.

"I baked some cookies," she said, "and thought you might like some."

"Say, thanks."

She handed me a plate with a dozen chocolate-chip cookies on them. Mrs. Goldman is a widow. She lived in this house for years with her husband and then decided to rent out the upstairs when he died. Lauren Bacall can only hope she looks as good at fifty as Mrs. Goldman does. In her crisp white blouse and blue skirt, she looked thirty-five. An envelope was tucked inside her right arm. "I'm also delivering this. I found it on the porch. I don't know why they didn't put it in the mailbox."

The phone rang. Mrs. Goldman smiled. "I'll let you catch that, Sam."

"Thanks for the cookies."

On the phone, Mom said, "I really had a good time at the game today, dear. I just wanted to thank you."

"My pleasure. Did you enjoy it?"

"Very much. Even though I didn't exactly understand a lot of what was going on. There are an awful lot of people on that field at one time. It gets confusing."

I smiled at the thought of Cliffie's cheer, "Kill those bastards!" If people would have shouted it, I think Mom would have mentioned it.

"Well, I'm glad you had a good time."

"You sound sort of rushed, dear. Is everything all right?"

"Just got in the door. Haven't even had time to get my sport coat off."

"Well, I'll let you go. But I just wanted to thank you for the tickets. That halftime show was great. I think that was my favorite part."

In the interest of good health, I fixed a peanut butter, mayo, and mustard sandwich before plowing into the cookies. That particular sandwich recipe probably doesn't sound all that good but you should give it a try.

I watched *Mike Hammer* with Darren McGavin, which was pretty good; and a *Lone Wolf* rerun with Louis Hayward. It was always sort of sad to see once-prominent actors have to resort to humiliating cheap-o TV shows. I wondered if fading TV stars worried about me the way I worried about them.

I'd inherited three cats—Tasha, Crystal, and Tess—from a girl who'd left them with me while she went to LA to become a star. She was waitressing in Redondo Beach and the cats were still mine. I'd never been what you call favorably disposed to felines but they'd grown on me.

They were nice enough to give me a portion of the bed around ten o'clock. The stuff on TV looked bad so I picked up the Steinbeck I was rereading, *In Dubious Battle,* and lost myself in the bleak rage of the early labor movement. For me it was his best book.

I was asleep by eleven-thirty. The phone rang at just before midnight according to the glowing hands of my alarm clock.

One of these nights it's going to be Natalie Wood telling me how lonely she is and that she's always wanted to see Black River Falls, Iowa, and couldn't she please come out and stay with me a few months.

It was Molly Blessing, who barely took time to introduce herself.

"I'm really scared, Mr. McCain."

"What about, Molly?"

"David got real drunk tonight."

"Where is he?"

"That's the thing. I'm not sure. And that's not the worst part, he's going to drag tonight."

"Where?"

"He wouldn't tell me. He said the cops always check out the spots everybody uses, so they were going to find a different place."

"Why didn't you go with him?"

"He said he was going to pick up that bitch Rita. I'm a lot better for him than Rita is. I try to get him to stop drinking and drag racing. She just encourages him to keeping doing them. I know I sound like a goody-two-shoes but if you really love somebody, Mr. McCain, shouldn't you want them to do the right thing?"

"I agree, Molly. But right now the important thing is to find David."

"He said you two had had an argument tonight. That you threatened to dump him."

"I got pretty mad, I guess."

"You're the only one he can rely on, Mr. McCain—if you didn't represent him, I don't know what would happen to him, I mean a lot of people think he killed Sara." Then, "I'm at the

A&W. At the phone booth. Could you pick me up and we'll go looking for David?"

"Yeah, maybe between us we can figure out where he went."

"He's so drunk, he's—"

"All we can do is hope for the best. I'll be there in fifteen minutes."

"I really appreciate this."

"I appreciate your calling, Molly. We need to stop him."

She waited on the corner for me. Even given the sudden autumnlike turn in the temperature, the A&W was crowded with cars, kids, and brave short-skirted carhops on roller skates.

Molly got in quickly. "I'm glad you put the top up. I'm kinda cold."

She wore a white sweater, jeans, and a rust-colored suede car coat that only enhanced the copper tones of her hair. "Do you mind if I smoke?"

"May I see some ID?"

She laughed. "Believe it or not, I still have to sneak around. At home, I mean. My father found a cigarette that had dropped out of my jacket one night. He grounded me for four nights and I was seventeen." She used the dash lighter, inhaled deeply, exhaled a long blue stream of smoke. "I don't even know where to start."

"I've been thinking. If he wants to avoid Cliffie, the two best places would be Graves Hollow or that road that runs by where the old closed mines are."

"Graves Hollow I'd thought of, too. But I forgot about the road by the old mines."

"I don't know where else to go so we may as well start there." Then, "If I were with him, I wouldn't let him race. Not as drunk as he is."

"How would you stop him? He's pretty hotheaded when he's drunk."

"I don't know—take his keys and throw them in the bushes if I had to."

"He'd just hot-wire his car."

"Then I'd take off his distributor cap and throw it in the bushes."

"Do you know what a distributor cap looks like?"

"Not exactly."

"Then how would you find it?"

"I'd ask somebody."

Neither of us could keep from smiling about that one.

"Or maybe I'd stop by a gas station and pick up one of those car guides," she said. "They'd have something in there about a distributor cap, wouldn't they?"

"Maybe it'd be easier to just take his tire iron and knock him out with it."

"Believe me, I've thought about it. He starts brooding about his childhood and drinking—he gets so irrational. I feel sorry for his aunts. He doesn't seem to appreciate how much time and love they put into raising him. He always says he was orphaned. But he wasn't. They saw to it he wasn't. That's the one trait I get tired of. The way he feels so sorry for himself. He didn't have it easy, I know that. But a lot of kids had it a lot worse." Then, "And she doesn't do anything to stop him when he gets drunk and crazy."

"She being Rita?"

"Of course. The lovely Rita. That bitch. I know I sound like a spoiled brat but I'm a lot better for him than Rita is. A lot better."

She obviously wanted me to agree with her. I didn't say anything.

Against the quarter-moon a scarecrow, arms flung wide, watched over a fallow cornfield and a small farmhouse with faint smoke eeling out of its chimney. Every once in a while the headlights would pick out empty beer cans and beer bottles scattered on the brown-grass sides of the road. These were the back roads where teenagers drank and went to first, second, or third base—or hell, maybe even hit a homer—depending on mood, pluck, and luck.

Graves Hollow was so named because of a graveyard that had been abandoned right after World War I. Between our war dead and two plagues of influenza, a new and much larger cemetery had been required. The dead were so long dead up on the hill that nobody alive could remember them, so nobody visited except kids who wanted to scare each other or put the make on their girlfriends. I've logged my share of make-out time in cemeteries. The cheap Freudian take on it all is that you're defying death with the affirmative act of lovemaking. The less fancy explanation is that it's a quiet place to get laid.

We drove the long, straight section of Hollow Road that local kids since the early 1920s had been using for drag racing. The west side of the road was steep and piney. The east side of the road was more fallow cornfields.

No sign of cars.

We headed for the old mines.

"Do you think he'll ever grow up?"

"Sure. Someday."

"How long will it take, do you think?"

"Offhand, I'd say three years, eleven months, and forty-two hours."

"I'm serious."

"I don't have any idea, Molly. It's easy for us to say he feels too sorry for himself. He hasn't had an easy life, even with all the stuff his aunts have done for him."

"That's why he treats women the way he does. That's what I think, anyway. He'll see some boy he's jealous of and then he'll take the kid's girl from him. Just for a week or so. But it makes him feel good, strong, you know what I mean?"

"Sure. And when he gets women to fall in love with him, it lets him, at least for a little while, think that he's as good as everybody else. Especially girls from the upper class."

"I read an article that said that for boys like him the conquest is everything. Then they have to move on to more conquests to make themselves feel good again." She tamped a cigarette from her pack. "That's what Sara was all about. I couldn't compete with her money."

She made a small fist. "God, I can get so mad at him—and yet I love him so much, too. I go around wanting to protect him all the time. Mostly from himself."

Right after the Civil War, coal mining came to our state and prospered until well into the next century, at which point, as if by divine edict, the mines began to be too expensive to operate. A few mines remained open but for the most part the miners moved on.

There was a moonscape ruggedness to the mined-out land now—stubby, mutated-looking pines dotted over hills of rocks and coarse grass on the sides of which were the boarded-up yaws of the mines themselves. A fair number of adventurous kids had been lost in those mines over the years, and about the same number of derelicts, fugitives, and madmen had hidden out in them. A small trestle bridge had washed out about two miles from the mining area about ten years ago and since the mine road wasn't used all that much anyway, the county supervisors decided to leave the land bridgeless.

Two miles of flat concrete were not anything the drag-racing teenager wanted to pass up. At first, this was the site Cliffie and his boys chose to patrol, but it became so heavily patrolled that the kids went elsewhere, leaving the mining road abandoned. But now it was the new places that Cliffie and his crew were patrolling. So little by little the dragsters were coming back to the mining road. Life is indeed a circle.

I'm a big fan of drive-in movie posters. I like the titles, too, such as *Hot Rods from Hell* and *Dragstrip Danger.*

The posters, and the movies they advertise, bring up the old argument of art imitating life—or life imitating art. Kids would've found out about racing their cars all by their lonesome. But it helped to have posters and movies that choreographed those events for them and showed them how to do it for the most powerful dramatic effect.

Makes you wonder what inspired kids in the Middle Ages, when there weren't any drive-ins.

As we reached the top of the hill a three-dimensional drive-in movie poster awaited us on the mining road below.

Twenty or so souped-up cars parked on the sides of the highway. The guys were divided into two styles—black leather jackets and jeans, or red James Dean jackets and jeans. The girls were inclined to wear tight skirts and even tighter sweaters and blouses. Some of them wore their boyfriends' jackets over their shoulders because of the cold. Most of them wore colorful neck scarves.

Everybody had a beer. Everybody had a cigarette. Everybody knew that they were in a movie of some kind.

There were two cars at the starting line—a fire-red 1950 Oldsmobile and David Egan's black Merc. The driver of the Olds had a blond hanging around his neck. From what I could see, Rita Scully was pouring coffee from a thermos into a cup for Egan.

"God, I hope this isn't liquor," Molly said.

"I'm sure it's coffee."

I pulled over to the shoulder and parked. The night air was clean and pure. Only as we got closer to the other cars along the road did the smells of gasoline and oil and cigarettes and beer begin to diminish the fresh prairie air.

We weren't popular with the drag-racing crowd. They let their faces show their displeasure. They didn't say a word, but smiles changed to sneers and conversations stopped to become practiced scowls. Just like in teenage gang movies.

But the movie images broke down when you saw them close up. All girls and boys in the juvenile delinquent movies were pretty and dramatic. But up close these kids had noses that were too big or small; a walleye here, a cross-eye there; a kid with oily black-heads, a kid with an overbite that was probably funny to every-body but him. A fat girl, a boy whose name-calling was marred by his lisp.

The eyes told you even more. In the movies, the actors had no lives but the plot. These kids had too much life and it was all there to see in the anger and cold amusement and sorrow of their eyes. Divorce, expulsion from high school, a year or two in reform school, low-wage jobs they'd toil at for long years, the scorn of their community, the anger that scared even them sometimes—it was all there to see and hear in the poses of anger and arrogance they struck as we moved deeper into the crowd.

Donny Hughes looked at me and said, "It's the fuzz."

Donny Hughes was the resident fool. Every group has one. He looked about eleven years old and had a black leather jacket so covered with zippers and chrome buttons that it was a parody, something a TV comic would wear in a skit about bikers. He was so short and so scrawny that the coat looked like a burden on him. He wore owl glasses and a blond duck's ass that would require six washings to get rid of all its butch wax.

He said, "Nobody invited the fuzz."

Molly said, "Shut up, Donny, you annoying little twerp."

I don't think you're supposed to talk to big bad bikers that way. Several people laughed.

Rita saw us before Egan did. Egan was so drunk I wasn't sure he was capable of seeing us. She whispered something to Egan as he was swearing at his cup for being too hot. He looked up. Frowned.

"What the hell're you doing here?" he said to me.

Rita glanced at Molly. "I hope you realize she's almost jailbait, McCain."

Molly said, "Rita, you can't let him race."

"What's this shit all about?" Egan said. "Get the hell out of here. I'm fine to race."

"I don't want him to race, either," I said to Rita.

"He's a big boy," Rita said.

"He sure isn't acting like it tonight," I said. "One of Cliffie's boys ever see him, he'd yank his license for a year. Maybe longer. And he'd have it coming, too."

That was the first time I noticed Kevin Brainard, a beefy, older guy who went six-two and easily better than two hundred pounds. He was drinking from a glass quart of Hamms. His hair was already thinning.

He wanted to intimidate and he did. You put five-five up against six-two and you don't have much of a contest.

"He was a hell of a lot drunker than this when he raced Mitch Callahan couple weeks ago," Brainard said.

"He was lucky, then," I said. "Maybe he won't be as lucky tonight."

"Who gave you the right to come out here, anyway?" Brainard said.

"Egan's my client."

"That don't cut shit out here, man. This strip belongs to us."

Drive-in dialogue. Real bad drive-in dialogue. He seemed unaware of just how bad, how self-concious.

I said to Egan, "Cliffie finds out you were drag racing and drunk on top of it, you'll go right to jail."

"Just get the hell out of here, McCain, and leave me alone. And take the princess with you."

"God, David, please listen to him—" Molly said, stepping toward him.

Rita came up in front of Molly. "Tell McCain here that in five seconds I'm telling Kevin to start breaking him in two. And I'm serious."

"But this is ridiculous," Molly said. "People don't do—"

But people *do* do. And people *do* do it all the time. They use clubs, fists, knives, guns, whatever it takes. Not in Molly's world but in the world at large—they *do* do it all the time.

We were in a movie and the inevitable scene of violence was upon us. I was getting my one and only close-up right now. I looked scared shitless was what I looked like. I didn't like to think of what Kevin Brainard could do to me.

Molly tried to walk around Rita but Rita wouldn't let her. She shoved Molly. "You take him, Kevin. I'll take her."

And then it started, that inevitable scene of violence I talked about.

Rock-and-roll radios blasting. Kids forming a circle around us. Rita twisting Molly around and getting her in a hammerlock. And Brainard hunching low and coming at me.

Fight scene—take one—the assistant director shouts.

And the camera starts rolling.

My dad taught me one thing about fighting when you're our diminuitive size. Fight dirty. Only chance you have. Leave the heroics to John Wayne and the movie stars.

So when Brainard came hulking toward me, his hands coming up and automatically forming clamps that would fit nicely around my throat, I steadied myself and hoped that my aim was as true as it usually was. He had to be in the right position and I had to be damned quick or the moment would be lost.

He came closer and closer.

Everybody was cheering him on. Some of the drive-in movie things they said were so stupid, I almost broke out laughing. Which I would've done if Brainard hadn't just spat in my face. He apparently believed in demolishing you only after he'd humiliated you. Still and all, even with spittle dripping down my forehead, "Kill him, daddy-o!" distracted the hell out of me.

"Daddy-o" was a word that was popular from approximately 1954 to 1958 or thereabouts. Slang expires just like bread and milk do at the supermarket.

But this was the wrong time to worry about the social faux pas of using dated slang. Because this huge, angry guy showing off for the crowd was about to seize my throat.

I fired my one and only weapon, which is the toe of my 8-D penny loafer. You can't tell right away if it worked. That's the only thing about getting somebody in the balls. It always takes a couple of seconds to register in the other guy's brain, as if his sac has to send his mind a telegram.

He kept coming, leaving me with the impression that my aim had been off. His clamplike hands groped for me—and then his face changed. It was as if he'd slipped on a new mask. If he'd been wearing rage, he was now wearing pain. Pain and misery and an anger he could only put into a few spluttering curse words.

He dropped to his knees, holding his crotch. He was momentarily immobilized.

I heard Molly scream. Rita still had Molly in a hammerlock, bending her over a car hood.

I started toward them but Egan reached them before I did. He put a quick hand on Rita's shoulder and said, "Let her go."

"She shouldn't be here."

"Let her go, Rita. Now."

Rita relented reluctantly. You could see that the pain didn't subside any for Molly. As she slumped against the car hood, I took her shoulder and gently tried to help her up. I knew better than to touch the arm Rita had been so expertly working on. Molly's eyes gleamed with tears as she began the millimeter-by-millimeter process of trying to straighten her arm out.

"You two get out of here," Egan said to my back. "A lot of these people here don't seem to like you. Anyway, I got a race."

His words were still slurred; he squinted to find focus.

Molly started to say something. I took her good arm and tugged her away from the car.

"Let's go," I said.

Then we were back to living our life inside that drive-in movie poster. There was a lot of posing and pouting, girls as well as boys, as I led Molly up the hill toward my car. Several of the hot-rodders revved their engines and their radios. It was a rock-and-roll moment, daddy-o.

"You really kicked Brainard hard," Molly said.

"Yeah."

"I'm glad."

"How's the arm?"

"I wish I would've been able to kick her. She's really mean." Her arm was at her side. She rubbed it with her good hand.

By the time we reached the top of the hill and the ragtop, the shouts below turned away from us and to the race.

We turned and watched. Rita positioned herself in the middle of the strip, arms raised above her head. She'd drop her arms and the cars would come screaming off the line.

"He's really going to do it, isn't he?"

"I'm afraid so, Molly."

"He could get killed."

"He's old enough to know what he's doing."

"I shouldn't have said what I said about him feeling so sorry for himself. I love him. I really do."

And then they were off.

We had a good place to watch. From here, the two dragsters were the size of huge toys.

They both fishtailed off the line, scarring the road with black tread, rubber crying like lost children. Molly's fingers dug into my wrist as we stood there in the nose-numbing wind, looking down into the darkness where headlights carved out an area that looked not unlike a cave. It was all primitive and it was all dangerous and it was all juvenile but I couldn't deny the excitement. I'd been in a lot of drag races myself. What's the point of having a hot car if you can't prove it's hot? But I'd never gone into a race drunk.

The black car and the red car stayed pretty close right up until the end and then the black car lurched ahead.

I realized what was going to happen before Molly did. From up here it was pretty easy to spot. The ones on the ground wouldn't realize it until it was over and too late.

The red car fought and fishtailed to a stop a few yards before the road ended, where the trestle bridge had once been.

Molly screamed, her nails ripping into my wrist.

What he did, David Egan, was overshoot the end of the road and hurtle into the air, smashing into the hard clay wall on the other side of the narrow river where the bridge had once been.

The explosion happened first. I'd seen Egan at the gas station not long ago. He probably had a full tank.

The explosion came in three quick segments, like bursts of railroad dynamite taking out a side of hill. A furious flare glared yellow-red-green-blue against the starry night sky, the spectacle of it hushing everybody for a terrible breath-held moment, the passenger's door ripping off and flying into the brightest depths of the explosion, glass and one of the taillights blowing up and out into the darkness.

And then the screams started from below. And people started running down the road toward the red car, whose driver was now outside his car and shouting something. He started running around in animal-crazy little circles.

Then the car disappeared into the river. Just vanished into the fast, moon-traced water.

And Molly was screaming and sobbing and shouting.

And all I could do was hold her and let her pound her little fists into me. I had no idea what to say to her. Or to myself.

PART 2

TWELVE

I N E V E R Y S M A L L T O W N there are one or two women who
shame everybody else with their virtue. It is not forced virtue or
contrived virtue and it does not necessarily have anything to do
with denominational religion, though it is the essence of Christ's
words before churches began twisting it to their own ends.

It's called decency. It's being kind, generous, and understanding
to those around you, even those you disagree with. It's not plaster
sainthood. This kind of virtue is capable of a tart comment but
never a mean one; of a disagreement but never one that questions
the other person's own virtue; and even a moment or two of
righteous anger when it sees a wrong. When the Goldmans first
moved here, somebody wrote JEW on their garage door. The Kelly
sisters went there immediately upon hearing about it, scrubbed
the word off, and gave the Goldmans a rhubarb pie they'd made
the night before. The Kelly sisters had grown up in the far west,
where Catholics had not always been welcome. They had a good
sense of what the Goldmans must have felt like.

Emma and Amy Kelly practiced such virtue every day. They
were the slender, white-haired, old maid aunts who had raised

David Egan after the death of his mother. They drove a 1939 Chevrolet that probably still hadn't topped 25,000 on the odometer and they dressed in the summery cotton dresses that they wore almost everywhere but Sunday mass. That called for the dark blue velveteen dresses they were known for when they took their place in the choir loft. They had beautiful voices; you could hear the song of the green hills of Gael in them. About the only time you heard them boast—and I can see their freckled girlish faces smiling as they'd say it—was when they boasted that they have never missed a Sunday mass, not even during the legendary flood of '43, for twenty-seven years running. They liked beer upon occasion, a "naughty" story upon occasion, and soap operas. Just as you could not convince a professional wrestling fan that his favorite sport was rigged, neither could you convince the Kelly sisters that soap operas were not lifelike. Their father was very much old country—true old country— spending his years as a key-and-lock man and a gunsmith. He'd often joined his daughters at church in singing hymns. He had a great Irish tenor voice.

By the time the Kelly sisters reached the old mine road tonight, more than one hundred people had gathered to watch divers bring up the body of David Egan and a winch begin to haul up what remained of his black Jimmy Dean Merc.

Cliffie's men let the Kelly sisters through the road block that had been set up at the top of the hill. Their sedan wasn't far from where I stood with Molly, who was in the process of working through her shock. I keep a pint of Old Grandad in my glove compartment for just such occasions. She'd had three hefty belts of it.

The Kelly sisters were dressed in dark zipper jackets, corduroy trousers, and golf hats that at any other time would have looked cute and jaunty. But this was not a night for cute and jaunty.

I walked over to them. They'd been on my long-ago paper

route. In the summer there was always a glass of Pepsi waiting for me when I stopped by to make my weekly collection. In the winter it was hot chocolate. And always, always there was the Kelly sisters' interest in your life. Conventional wisdom said that the Kelly sisters took such interest in the lives of the young people around them because they'd never had kids of their own. And I suspect that was true. But it made their interest no less valuable. You said things to the Kellys you might not say to your parents— no dark secrets, you understand, but daydreams most older folks would dismiss as foolish. Things like that.

Emma's arthritic hand took mine and she said, "We hadn't seen him since just after lunch. Was he drunk, Sam?"

They didn't want lies. They'd lived hard working-class lives and while they needed the same number of delusions and hopeless hopes we all needed to survive, at a moment like this they wanted the truth.

"He was pretty bad off, Emma," I said.

Amy was the one who reacted. She crossed herself. She was praying for his soul.

"Did anybody else get hurt?" Emma said.

"No. The other kid stopped in time."

"Thank God," Emma said. "At least it was just himself."

The hardness of her tone surprised me. Amy put a trembling hand to her eyes to wipe away tears. But Emma's eye were dry, the blue of them cold.

She said, "Did they recover the body?"

"Yes. The ambulance took it away."

Amy winced and brought her shoe up—an oxford—and squeezed it. "Ruined my new white Keds this afternoon on the side of the house. I've got them hanging on the wash line. Hope it'll get the oil out." Then, "But who cares about my shoes at a time like this?"

She was getting disoriented, which is how some people deal with bad news.

Molly came up. She started toward Emma but Emma pulled back abruptly, as if a plague victim had tried to touch her. "This isn't a good time for your whining, Molly. And tell Rita the same thing. I don't want to hear from either one of you for a long time. Maybe never."

She was trying to deal with it her way, I realized now. Amy was somewhat dithering. Emma wanted to be strong and in this instance being strong meant measuring your words and not giving in to the moment.

"Sam, will you come over in the morning after mass?" Emma said.

"Of course."

"You don't want to go over there and look?" Amy said to her sister.

"For what? So we'll have some more bad memories?"

I'd never heard Emma speak to Amy this way. It wasn't a barroom brawl but for two loving sisters it was certainly a cold question.

Amy looked at me, embarrassed. They weren't public women. They left that to the Irish menfolk, the brawlers and bellyachers and bullies with all the storms they dragged around with them.

"Let's go," Emma said to Amy.

"But we've only been here a few minutes."

"I don't want to be here anymore," Emma said. She touched her sister's arm. "I shouldn't have spoken that way to you. I'm sorry."

"It's all right, Emma," Amy said. "We each have different ways of dealing with things is all."

"See you in the morning, Sam," Emma said.

"Good night, Sam," Amy said.

"Good night," I said.

I heard it before I saw it. And when I heard it I wasn't sure what it was. Just some kind of whimper, some kind of curse.

Somebody shouted.

Something heavy and fast-moving slammed into me. Rita had just jumped on Molly's back. She had a handful of that lovely coppery hair and she was jerking Molly's head back and forth.

I returned the favor, grabbing a handful of Rita's hair and yanking on it hard enough to make her cry out. "Let her go, Rita."

She wouldn't let go. I wound more of her hair around my hand and jerked all the harder. This time she screamed. And let go.

When she was free of Molly, I shoved her away.

"You happy you came out here and ruined his night for him, Molly?" Rita screamed at her. "You and this asshole lawyer of yours? Maybe if you two hadn't given him all your grief he wouldn't have smashed his car up. Maybe he was so mad at you two he couldn't think straight."

We all need somebody to blame. Maybe in the future there'll be something called a blame robot, a little metal guy that follows you around and takes the blame for anything you do wrong or anything fate decides to dump on you.

For Rita, Molly was handy. Her accusation made no sense. But it didn't need to make any sense.

Molly slipped her arm through mine. "Will you take me home?"

"Oh," Rita said. "Isn't that so sweet? Maybe she'll sleep with you if you're real nice to her, McCain."

Brainard came over. Slid his arm around Rita's shoulder. The hurt I'd put on him had apparently faded. He said, "C'mon, Rita. These two ain't worth botherin' with."

His gentleness surprised me. Guy his size, his temperament, being capable of such a quiet, soothing tone. Was it because Egan was dead or because Brainard had more feelings for Rita than he usually let on?

Molly led me away.

Halfway to her place, she said, "I've really got a headache."

"If it's any comfort, the way I grabbed her, I'm sure Rita's got one, too."

"I never liked her. She was always sneaking around with David behind my back. But I've never hated her the way she hates me." Then, "I haven't really cried yet."

"You could've fooled me."

"Oh, that was nothing. I was inhibited by all the people around."

"When you get home then—"

"When I get home I'll have to go through the Inquisition. And then they'll gloat."

"I assume you're talking about your parents?"

"Could you turn the heat on?"

"Sure."

"Thanks. And yes, I'm talking about my parents. They'll try to hide it. Their gloating. They'll say how sorry they are about him dying. But they'll be relieved. He won't be around to bother them anymore. Meaning he won't be around to bother me. Anymore. My father hated him. Really. Deep, deep hatred. I was a virgin until I met David. He's the only boy I've ever slept with. I made the mistake of telling my mom that. Supposedly in confidence. But she told my father, of course. I really think he's jealous. He just got crazy. He got drunk for several nights in a row and then he'd come upstairs and start screaming at me. He even called me a whore a couple of times. My mom really got scared."

"Did he ever confront David?"

"Once. One night he got really drunk and went looking for him. My mom says he keeps a loaded forty-five—his old army pistol—in the nightstand drawer. She went to look for it but it wasn't there. She was afraid Dad would kill him or something. The whole night was crazy. She couldn't call Cliffie because he'd tell everybody that Dad went off with a gun looking for David. Fortunately, she didn't have to tell Cliffie anything. Cliffie saw Dad weaving down the street and pulled him over. Made him park the car and then brought him home. Dad didn't say anything about David or the gun apparently. If Dad weren't so important, Cliffie would've run him in. Anyway, he didn't get to David."

My headlights pierced the leafy darkness of her narrow street. The eyes of raccoons gleamed silver in the shrubs and undergrowth. The family dog began yapping before I was even halfway up the drive.

When I pulled up, she leaned over and kissed me on the cheek. "I wish you were younger or I were older." She was all coppery hair and heartbroken smile. Egan had been a fool.

"Or you were shorter or I were taller."

"We're a pair." Then, "You know what I'm doing, don't you?"

"Stalling for time before you have to go inside."

"You're very perceptive."

"What scares you the most, facing your parents or being alone in your room?"

"Being alone. Because I'm going to fall apart."

"Maybe that's what you need," I said. "Falling apart. Then when you wake up you'll be stronger."

"Rita could've stopped him tonight. This is her fault, you know."

"Kiddo," I said, not up for another flaying of her romantic rival, "it's time for you to go inside."

I drove around for an hour. This time Saturday night there would still be kids out cruising. The hard drunks would be done for the night, passed out or punched out or puked out. Only the melancholy ones would be left. They'd had dates and the dates had to be home at midnight and now they were cruising alone, melancholy for the girls they'd just dropped off, because they loved them so damned much; or melancholy because they were so damned afraid they would lose them, secretly reviewing all their inadequacies and just hoping the girls never found out about them for themselves. They would hit the highway and turn up the rock and roll and let the moon shine on them with its ancient solitary soothing truths.

The local TV stations always signed off at midnight, even on weekends. Nothing's lonelier than the keen of a test pattern.

I climbed into bed shortly after one, read six pages, and fell thankfully into a deep and dreamless sleep. I went through all the usual tussles with the cats, Tasha deciding at some point during the night to examine my face the way a dermatologist would, her purring almost as loud as her snoring; little Crystal head-butting my arm so I'd give her a sleepy scratch; and Tess biting my foot when I made the mistake of trying to move it so I could get comfortable. I'd slept with my boyhood dog for years so I knew all about how to sleep with, around, and through the experience of pets in the same bed.

It was darktime when the phone woke me. No particular time or place or world. Just darktime.

My weary hand reaching out for the telephone on the nightstand. My weary ear feeling the cold receiver against it. My weary mind trying to make sense of the words. He or she was stingy with words. A regular haiku master. I say he or she because it was either a female talking through a handkerchief or a male talking through a handkerchief and sliding his voice up an octave, not quite falsetto.

"It wasn't an accident."

No emotion. No elaboration.

"You hear me? It wasn't an accident."

THIRTEEN

NEXT MORNING, I WENT out there even though there was no reason to do it. I went up to the edge of the crevice where the bridge had ripped away and I just stood there. It was a cool, sunny, autumn Sunday and even this far away from the center of town you could hear the bells of the Catholic church. The red limestone wall on the opposite side of the river was like a bulletin board of bits and pieces of Egan's Merc, bits and pieces that were strewn everywhere. A chrome headlight rim, bent and busted, caught the sunlight. A foot-long length of tire was somehow adhered to the wall. What appeared to be a section of bumper stuck straight out. The front of the car had left an outline in the limestone. Parts of the display were oily from impact. There were violent rents and deep gouges but they didn't leave any discernible pattern.

I had no idea what I was looking for. Maybe I wasn't looking for anything. Maybe that phone call had made me suspicious enough to come out here, even though the chances were it was a prank. There are people who enjoy making miserable events even more miserable for those involved. I don't understand people who admire communism, I don't understand people who hurt children, I don't understand people who rob and cheat old people, I don't understand White Sox fans. And I especially don't understand people who find human grief something to exploit for laughs or profit. Someday I'm going to build my own private death row and I'm going to put all these people in it. Except for the White Sox fans. Following that team is punishment enough. No incarceration required.

I drove back down to the starting line. The blue air was alive with pheasants. You could watch them take fragile flight, their elegant colors vivid above the cornfields and the meadows. In another week it would be legal for hunters to put their rifles and shotguns on them and blow the shit out of them. From all the gunfire in the surrounding hills it sounded as if at least a few of the brave and intrepid hunters were already blasting away. Those damned pheasants are mean.

The area around the starting line was a mess of crushed beer cans, crumpled cigarette packages, pop cans, smashed bottles, empty potato chip packages. But when you looked away from the debris, looked up at the smoky autumn hills, everything was clean and coherent, and the death of a young man last night seemed not obscene but impossible.

I wasn't looking for it when I found it. I walked right past it, recognizing it for what it was, of course, but not connecting it to Egan or last night.

I was just walking back to my car when I happened to see the trail of it glistening there, a gleaming snake that had already claimed its victim—a gleaming trail of oil.

I walked over to the snake and measured its lengths in steps. The snake extended well beyond my desire to count off its length.

I wasn't sure what it meant. There might be a harmless explanation. Or a harmful one. Extremely harmful.

It was getting hotter. I went over and put the top down on my ragtop. I headed back to town.

People clog the churches on Sunday morning, so I always feel self-conscious when I'm tooling past a church and the congregation is gathered on the steps to congratulate the minister on another dynamic sermon—the congregation always gives you the look it reserves for burglars and heathens.

I was hoping to find Egan's smashed-up car at the DX station where I trade.

It sat in front of an open bay waiting for its autopsy. The motor might be salvageable—probably was—as well as some of the custom accoutrements that private owners would pay decent money for.

Jay Norbert was looking it over and nodding his head in rhythm to whatever his customer was saying.

The car itself was a great alien metal beast to be pondered and studied. A lot of people would want to know what had gone wrong. Had it been the car or Egan or both?

The customer walked away just as I approached. Jay had just gotten out of the army. He'd been a good mechanic when he went in; he was an even better one now that he was out. He was a skinny twenty-two-year-old who was already losing his hair. He always kept his uniform spotless. His boss had opened another gas station across town and put Jay in charge of this one. A doctor in a nearby town had done some questionable things during the pregnancy of Jay's wife; that was why I knew his story. We were suing the doc.

"Sonofabitch," Jay said. "There isn't enough left here to haul to the junkyard."

"The poor bastard."

"I didn't like him but I sure wouldn't wish this on him."

"Why didn't you like him?"

"He came on to Marie one day." Marie being his wife, a pretty farm girl. "Right in front of me, too. I started to say something but Marie dragged me away. Was hard workin' on his car when he came in."

"That's what I wanted to talk to you about."

"Oh, what's that?"

"His car. I was wondering if you'd check something for me."

He smiled. "Cliffie was in. He's already got it figured out, he says."

"Really? This should be good."

"Friday night Egan kills the girl, see, and Saturday night he's so guilty he gets all gooned up and then runs his car right off the road. Case closed."

"Man, that Cliffie. When he puts that brain of his to use, stand back and watch the sparks fly."

He laughed. "I suppose it could've happened that way."

"He didn't kill her."

I was just walking back to my car when Donny Hughes pulled up. His heavily chromed black leather jacket was just as inevitable as his waterfall blond ducktail. "Holy shit. No wonder he died." His entire face tightened as he looked at the remains of Egan's Merc.

"That's right. You keep on drinking and drag racing, that could be you."

He stayed in his street rod, an elbow on the open window of the driver's side. "Wonder how Rita's doin'?"

"I wouldn't bother her right now."

"Things may change, McCain. With Egan dead, maybe she'll

see how much I dig her. I buy her gifts all the time. Just bought her a pair of desert boots and a new green sweater. You should see that sweater on her."

"I wouldn't move in on her just yet, Donny. I think the mandatory grieving time is something like an hour and a half in this state."

"Hey, McCain, I didn't mean—"

I waved him off and went to my car. It never takes long for the "good friends" to move in on the spoils.

Scrambled eggs, blueberry muffins, three strips of perfectly cooked bacon, orange juice—this was the breakfast Emma and Amy Kelly had fixed for me.

Theirs was an immigrant Irish house, a tiny white clapboard box on a tiny lot with a tiny garage on its back edge. A well-scrubbed living room, dining room, kitchen, bathroom, and two bedrooms packed with doilies, small statues of the Virgin and assorted saints, an eleven-inch TV screen, and framed paintings of Christ that managed to be sad and somehow lurid at the same time. We ate in the dining room on a table that smelled of its new oilcloth covering with a decades-old record player scratching out Irish jigs from the living room.

Emma looked as composed, even cold, as she had on the highway last night. Amy's eyes were red and ruined and her flesh was gray.

Emma said, "I suppose you've heard what that stupid ass Cliffie is saying."

"That it was suicide?"

Emma nodded. "He isn't Catholic. He doesn't understand. For a Catholic to take his own life—"

"—eternal damnation," Amy said.

"He got drunk and wrecked his car. That's all that happened. And he didn't kill that Sara Griffin girl, either. He loved her."

"That's exactly what he said? That he loved her?"

"He told both of us that," Emma said. "And she was the only girl he'd ever said that about."

"When did he say that?"

She looked at Amy. "Tuesday?"

"Monday, I think," Amy said. "It was right after 'The Lucy Show.'"

"You and your 'Lucy Show'," Emma said. She reached over and patted her sister's hand. "We each have our favorite shows and argue about which of them is best. I like Jackie Gleason."

"He's not a very good Catholic is what I read in the papers," Amy said. "He's married but he runs around on his wife all the time."

"They're separated," Emma said.

"That doesn't matter in the eyes of the church," Amy said. "He still shouldn't be running around on her."

I wondered if Jackie Gleason's ears were burning. His sex life was being discussed with some force by two elderly Catholic ladies in rural Iowa.

"David wanted to marry Sara," Amy said.

"He treated her differently from the others."

"How so?"

"For one thing," Amy said, "he had to chase her rather than the other way around."

"And she was troubled, too, the poor thing," Emma said. "Her father putting her in that mental place. And those electroshock treatments. There was a thing on TV about them. They're really scary to watch."

"Imagine what it's like to go through them," Amy said.

"Anyway, we want you to have something, Sam," Emma said.

And from the pocket of her apron she took a small white envelope and placed it carefully next to my coffee cup. "This is the best we can do. But we'll have more for you in the future."

Inside the envelope was one hundred dollars in denominations of twenty.

"What's this?"

"We're hiring you," Emma said.

"To do what?"

"Prove that David didn't kill poor Sara."

"And that he didn't commit suicide," Amy said.

"He was like our son, Sam. He had a pretty rough reputation and a lot of it he deserved. But he doesn't deserve to be remembered as a murderer and a suicide."

"And you know Cliffie, Sam," Amy said. "At mass this morning, Mrs. Corroon said that Mrs. Kerry's husband, Earl, saw Cliffie at the Bluebird Café this morning and Cliffie was telling everybody how he'd wrapped everything up already. David killed Sara and committed suicide."

"Yeah, I heard that particular bit of Cliffie wisdom myself. But I can't take this money."

"Why not?"

"Because if I do I'll fall off the wagon again."

"What wagon?" Amy said.

"He means he'll start drinking again," Emma said. "But since when did you have a drinking problem?"

"Couple years now. Every time I get my hands on any money, I go on a bender."

Emma smiled at her sister. "He doesn't want to take our money because he thinks we're poor."

"Why, we're not poor, Sam," Amy said. "Even after we took

this out of the jar we keep in the basement—we just don't trust banks since the Depression and all—we've got seventy-five dollars left. And people with seventy-five dollars aren't exactly poor, you know."

They were regular John D. Rockefellers, they were.

"How about this? I have my own reasons to work on this."

"It's Judge Whitney, isn't it?" Emma said.

"Is it true she hates Catholics?" Amy asked.

"Yes, but don't take it personally," I said. "She hates just about everybody."

"Judge Whitney wants to prove that Cliffie's wrong so she wants you to find out what happened, am I right?"

"You're absolutely right. According to her she wants me to 'humiliate' him."

"Cliffie's so stupid, I doubt he even knows it when he's being humiliated," Emma said. Then crossed herself. "My Lord, listen to me, will you? Saying things like that about the poor man. The Lord saw fit to make him stupid for a reason only the Lord himself can understand. It's not for me to question the Lord's reasons for things."

"We're just mad because he's telling everybody that David killed Sara and then killed himself."

"I don't blame you. I'm mad, too. And I intend to start proving he's wrong."

"When do you think you'll start, Sam?"

I glanced at my Timex, drained the last of my coffee, and stood up. "How about right now?"

I went to the grocery store for milk and cat food, the cigar store for cigarettes and Sunday papers from the biggest cities I could find, and finally to the DX for another peek at the wreck of

Egan's black Merc. Jay Norbert was on his haunches with a flash-light, trying to find what I'd asked him to look for inside the tangled metal.

Then I stopped by the office for some papers I'd forgotten. I was a couple feet from my interior office door when I heard the crying. I'd heard her cry so many times before, I knew who it was immediately.

She cried the day she got a bad hairdo down at the House of Beauty styling salon, she cried the day her teacher informed her that she was getting an F in typing, she cried the day it was announced that Dick and Darla and not John and Jeanie had won the *American Bandstand* dance contest.

But mostly what she cried about was Turk, the eighteen-year-old hotshot who'd dropped out of high school so he could "like, you know, make some bread," which he was currently doing by working at Suds City, the local car wash. To be fair, I don't sup-pose he meant to be as irritating as he was. He wasn't posing as Jimmy Dean or Marlon; he was irritating all on his own, one of those dumb, puppy-dog kids who will always be seventeen years old. Turk was Jamie's boyfriend and Jamie was my secretary, loaned to me by her father in lieu of the money he owed me for representing him in a boundary dispute with his neighbor. I wonder if Jamie isn't the vessel of his retribution. I'd lost the case for him.

Jamie was the prototype for every teenage girl depicted on the covers of paperbacks where the term "jailbait" is used, a bouncy, giggly and vastly earnest girl who could, at her most dangerous, turn the simple act of boiling an egg into a kitchen explosion that would flatten the house.

I like Jamie. I don't know why I like her, I don't even want to like her, and no, it isn't that heartbreaking teenage body of hers, either. It's her sincerity, I guess. She's sincere about everything, and to a fault. You don't find many people like that outside of convents for cloistered nuns or the third floor of asylums where they keep the violent ones.

"Oh, Mr. C," she sobbed when I walked in. "My mascara."

True, she did have little black snakes wriggling down her nicely shaped cheeks. But they were sincere little black snakes. The Mr. C reference is one she picked up from the *Perry Como* TV show, where all the dancers call him "Mr. C." Jamie thinks this is pretty cool. Someday she'll realize that because my last name is McCain, I should be "Mr. M."

She wore a brown sweater that would inspire a rush to cold showers by middle-aged men throughout these United States, and a pair of jeans that defined the rest of that paperback body. She was also smoking a cigarette, something I'd never seen her do before. The cigarette was parked on the edge of a Camel cigarette tin ashtray right next to my framed photo of the sad-sweet face of Shemp, my favorite of the Three Stooges. Himmler of Black River Falls decorated my place right before they sent him up for the third time on the charge of offending the public taste.

"Gosh," I said, "is everything all right at home?"

"Everything's fine," she said with that kind of girly forlornness that teeters self-consciously between tragedy and comedy. "At home, I mean, everything's fine. But everything's not fine between Turk and me."

"Good old Turk. What'd he do now?"

She sniffled. "He misspelled my name."

Coming from a girl who has often misspelled my name on letters—even though the correct spelling appears in the letterhead at the top—this was quite an accusation.

"I'm sure he didn't do it on purpose, Jamie."

She was bawling over Turk misspelling her name?

She sniffled some more. "It's just that it's forever."

"What's forever?"

"The tattoo." Said as if I were a mind reader and should have known what she was talking about.

"Ah," said I, "the tattoo." The reason for her misery was coming clear.

Only Turk could have pulled this baby off.

"Let me see if I can reconstruct this."

"It's terrible, Mr. C. Just horrible."

"Turk got drunk."

"Yes. Very, very drunk."

"And somebody gave him a tattoo."

"That stupid Phil Craper."

"And Phil was drunk, too."

"Phil's always drunk. He's a wino."

"And so Phil is as bad a speller as Turk. And when they went to put the tattoo on they wrote—"

"J-a-m-m-i-e. 'I love Jammie' it says. With a heart."

"And the tattoo is on—"

"—his shoulder. And you know how he likes to walk around without his shirt on. People'll laugh at it when they see it. They'll think Turk is stupid."

"Gee, I can't imagine that."

She shook her cute head miserably and stared off at a fate that not even her worst enemy could have contrived. "And people'll start calling me Jammie, Mr. C." A sob. "Sometimes I feel like my life is just over." She raised teary blue eyes to me. "Do you ever feel like that?"

"Six or seven times a day."

She didn't smile. "Jammie. I just can't believe he could be that dumb. Even when he was drunk."

The phone rang.

She watched it as if it were going to do something obscene. "It's him."

"Turk?"

"Uh-huh."

It rang and rang.

"Aren't you going to answer?"

"I'll let him suffer."

"You know, Jamie, it could just possibly be for me. I mean, this is a law office. Not a huge or very successful law office. But a law office nonetheless."

She shrugged, unfazed by my pompous little speech. "I can tell by the ring it's Turk. It just sounds a certain way."

I saw the file folder I'd forgotten to take home. I'd left it on my desk.

"I think I'll just pick this up and go, Jamie."

The ringing phone was going to make me psychotic any minute now.

"You're sure it's Turk?"

"Sure I'm sure, Mr. C," she said, sounding a little peeved. "Can't you tell by the sound of that ring?"

FOURTEEN

WHENEVER JUDGE ESME ANNE Whitney wore jodhpurs, she always recalled—Galouise cigarette in one hand and snifter of brandy in another—how when she was a lass of fourteen in a boarding school so refined none of the girls there so much as went to the bathroom, Noel Coward appeared and took her and another girl horseback riding on a mild April afternoon.

There were a couple of things wrong with this story and it wasn't, believe it or not, the Noel Coward part. She really had met famous people of all sorts in her lifetime. The rich are, you see, a very special and very private club. They don't use anything as vulgar and common as a secret handshake to identify each other. As near as I can figure out the code is conveyed through a complicated series of rapid eye movements that only they understand. Sort of like the flickering light codes our war ships used during World War II.

The parts that bothered me about this old chestnut of hers was (A) the appearance of the horse and (B) the idea of another girl being present.

Judge Esme Anne Whitney is terrified of horses, will not get within yards of one of them. She'd once dragged me to a horse show to which her friend the governor had invited her and whispered to me, "God, don't people ever get sick of seeing these creatures emptying their bowels." Judge Whitney on a horse? I have my doubts.

As for another girl going along to keep Esme Anne and Mr. Coward company, impossible. No way would Esme Anne Whitney share such a moment. She would want herself to be the only one with bragging rights to this particular tale.

"Dear Noel," Judge Whitney said this afternoon, seated on the veranda of her mansion, the maid, a masochist named Nell O'Bannion, having just delivered up another bottle of brandy, "dear, dear Noel." She took a dramatic puff of her Galouise—Bette Davis had once taken acting lessons from the judge—"dear, dear Noel."

Then she said, not being great at changing subjects with any grace: "I want his face rubbed in it this time, McCain."

"You want dear, dear Noel Coward's face rubbed in it?"

"My Lord, McCain, pay attention will you? Just because you're short doesn't mean you have to be stupid, too. I want Cliffie's face rubbed in it."

"Ah. Cliffie."

She had her rubber band ready to go. I wondered if Nell O'Bannion had brought her the rubber bands along with her first bottle of brandy. She set down her snifter and her Galouise long enough to load up her forefinger and thumb and fire at me. She was damned good at her little game. She did a double fake—pretended to be firing from the left and then suddenly shifting to the right and, as I moved my head to the left, surprised me by moving back to the left again. The rubber band hung off my nose momentarily and then dropped to the table. She had a dead aim.

A squirrel sitting on the edge of the patio watched me with great disdain. His expression seemed to question why I didn't have more self-respect than to sit with a half-fried, jodhpur-wearing, horse-loathing Eastern lady of vast wealth and even vaster disdain for common folk like me. I should've told the squirrel that it was none of his damned business. Instead I explained (don't knock telepathy until you try it) that I needed the money. I made a pittance from my law practice. I earned a modest living by working as Judge Whitney's investigator.

I watched the squirrel romp off in the direction of the surrounding forest, diving in and out of the frothy colorful waves of crisp autumn leaves. He had an enviable life.

She inhaled half her Galouise and then took a long drink from her snifter. There was a cold beauty in the fine-boned lines of her face. She'd had innumerable husbands and lovers but always ended up alone. In my way, I liked her in a complicated and melancholy sort of fashion, at least in those moments when my hands weren't aching to wrap themselves around her elegant throat.

She said, "Jack Coyle."

"All right, I'll play along. Jack Coyle."

"A social worker who was involved in a case I presided over a while back told me about a rumor she'd heard."

"Involving Jack Coyle."

"My, you're quick today."

"I thought we might be talking about dear, dear Noel again."

"I'm handing you some important information and you sit here drinking my brandy making fun of me. You really are a dunce, McCain."

"Jack Coyle. Tell me."

More wine. More Galouise.

"This is unconfirmed, of course."

"My favorite kind of rumor."

"This particular caseworker had worked as a high school counselor at one time. And one of the students she saw was Sara Griffin."

She'd hooked me. School counselor. Sara Griffin. Jack Coyle. Whatever it was, it was bound to be juicy.

"Sara was going through a very difficult time."

"This was before or after her folks put her in that asylum?"

"Just before. Anyway, the counselor told me that several times Sara referred to this 'older man' she was seeing. She never used a name. But one evening the counselor was out at the state park with her kids—they were having a picnic—and down by the boathouse she saw Jack Coyle and Sara Griffin. They weren't doing anything untoward, you understand. They were standing there talking. But then they got into some kind of argument and Sara ran away in tears. She said that Jack Coyle stalked off after Sara. She didn't know what happened after that. She had to get back to her kids."

"I don't know what to say."

She smiled. "I couldn't wait to tell you this, McCain. I wish I could get a picture of your face at this moment. You look absolutely shocked."

"I am absolutely shocked." I decided to give her the pleasure of telling me something I already knew. "But it's just rumor."

She smiled again. "Cliffie's in way over his head this time, McCain." She said this with the relish of deep hatred.

"Yes, he is."

"He's going all over town saying that the case is closed and that David Egan was the killer. But we're going to prove otherwise, aren't we, McCain?"

"We sure are."

"This doesn't mean I suspect Jack Coyle."

"No, of course not."

"But," she smirked, "I'd sure love to have a picture of his face when you ask him about poor Sara Griffin. Now take care of this for me will you, McCain?"

"I'll do my best," I said, standing up.

The cold beauty smiled again but without any hint of merriment. "That may not be enough on a matter like this, McCain. I'd suggest you aim a little higher than your best."

Walking to my car, I came up with at least eighteen great cracks to make about middle-aged society women who wore jodhpurs but were terrified of horses. I couldn't, of course, say any of them out loud.

It was a high school sort of date. Back then I would've made sure that my ducktail was combed flat, that I was smiling so much my lip muscles hurt, that I appeared manly enough to please the father and trustworthy enough to please the mother. If one of them asked me what I planned to do with my life, I generally said that I hoped to become a doctor and work on a cure for cancer; and if they inquired of my extracurricular activities, it being obvious that athletics did not number among them, I told them that I spent most of my time stocking shelves for the nuns down at the Pantry for the Poor they ran. If they were Protestant parents, I said that I stocked shelves at the Martin Luther Poverty Center. In other words, it was all Pat Boone bullshit.

Mrs. Dennehy, her husband being understandably absent because of his death, said, "So how is your law practice going, Sam?"

We were in the living room. Brett Maverick was cheating somebody at poker on the TV screen and Fred, their black Lab, was stinking up my hand with his tongue. Linda was "just about ready." Or so she'd called out from some secret place outside the small but comfortably furnished living room. Mrs. Dennehy was of a different generation of Irish Catholics than Emma and Amy Kelly so she didn't have quite as many framed paintings of Jesus on the walls. And Jesus wasn't quite so pretty as in the older paintings. The more modern ones showed a Jesus who didn't look like a pushover for just any sob story you decided to lay on him. There were strands of palm from Palm Sunday, to be sure, placed behind the two framed paintings of the Virgin on the wall but not nearly the number my Mom had in the bedroom she shared with my dad all these years. The Pope was nowhere to be found.

"My law practice is going just fine," I said, thinking of Jamie or Jammie, depending on your taste and level of literacy. "I have a new secretary and business has really picked up."

"Do you still work for Judge Whitney?"

"Yes, part-time," I said, "though as my business picks up, I work for her less and less." I plan to be a doctor someday, Mrs. Dennehy, and search for a cure for cancer. After that, I plan to rid our planet of racism in all its ugly forms.

"That's good. No offense, Sam, but she's pretty hard to take sometimes. She gave a talk at one of our church suppers and she kept calling us 'you people.' It was like she couldn't bring herself to say the word 'Catholic.'"

I smiled. Lord, how I smiled. "I think it's safe to assume she won't become a papist anytime soon."

"Mom asks a lot of questions, doesn't she?"

"Not a lot."

"Well, quite a few."

"Quite a few, maybe," I said, "but not a lot."

She punched me gently on the arm. "You're really on your best behavior tonight."

I laughed. "Wait till later."

The restaurant was all dark wood, red leatherette booths, candles inside red glass, waitresses in black nylon uniforms, and a trio that apparently hadn't heard of any music hipper than Lawrence Welk. But they played slow songs and slow songs were what I wanted to hear. It was so dark in there I thought maybe I should've worn one of those miner's hats with the flashlights built into them.

We ate and drank, steaks and whiskey, the whiskey coming from the pint in my suitcoat. Hard liquor is available here only in state-run stores. But Cliffie is pretty understanding of people who bought restaurant setups and used their own bottles.

I went easy on the booze. She drank more than I expected, enough in fact to have some minor difficulty getting her tongue to form words exactly.

"I can't drink at all."

"You're doing fine," I said.

"I'm just so nervous."

"Everything's fine."

"I'm afraid I'm going to hyperventilate."

"You want to go outside?"

She shook her head. "No, I just have to grow up."

I wasn't quite sure what she meant by that but I had my suspicions.

"You think we could dance, Sam?"

We danced. She was good. She felt right in my arms, too. A lot of times they don't. She felt right in other ways, too, that small earnest freckled face of hers so prairie-girl scrubbed and prairie-girl smart.

We didn't bother going back to our booth for nearly half an hour. We just danced. And what we couldn't give voice to our bodies spoke of. Sex, to be sure, but also comfort and care and memories that stretched all the way back to kindergarten when we'd tasted white paste for the first time and learned how to color inside the lines.

"You're going to ask me to go back to your place tonight, Sam. And I'm going to say yes because I really want to go. Because I've been thinking of you all the time since Friday night. But I'm really scared. This has to move very, very slowly, Sam. I'm not feeling very female after the operation and maybe it's just not going to be worth it for you. In the long run, I mean. Maybe nothing will ever come of it for you."

"You didn't need to say any of that stuff, you know."

"I just had to make it official."

She had one more drink before we left.

"They like you," I said, after coming out of the john and seeing how my three cats had made themselves comfortable pressed against her on either side. Tess of course sat in her lap. Tess believes in the divine right of cats. To hell with all that jazz about the divine right of kings.

"You like a drink?" I said.

"No, thanks. I wouldn't mind using the bathroom, though. I just don't want to offend your cats by making them move."

"The only thing that offends these cats is when they run out of food."

While she was tending to business, I put on the Bobby Darin album he did live at the Copa. When she came back, she sat down, turned off the table lamp, took my arm, put it around her shoulder, and then snuggled up to me.

"How's that for being forward?" she said.

"I'm shocked, you hussy."

We sat. I knew enough not to make any grand moves; I also knew enough not to talk. Darin was especially good with the

Cole Porter songs, gave them a rawness you don't associate with Porter. Maybe even gave the lyrics a little more depth.

She kissed me and it was one hell of a kiss. Another feeling of comfort. Sometimes you can like a lady a whole lot but you just don't work well together sexually. Kissing's pretty important. We fit together perfectly.

It went on a long time and then she eased me away with a small deft hand and said, "I wasn't sure I could ever feel like that again."

We nuzzled and snuggled and then we snuggled and nuzzled and then we snuzzled and nuggled and it was great.

On the other side of the screen door a dog and an owl and a Hank Williams album communed with us and the night.

"You know what?" she said.

"You'd better go."

"I didn't know you were a mind reader."

"I want this to work, Linda."

"So do I."

"So you'd better go."

She kissed me again and certain of my body parts reacted by standing straight up and saluting.

"Do you believe in God?" she asked when I was slipping her coat on.

"Most of the time."

"That's sort of how I am. In the hospital it was a real struggle. My mom and everybody would bring me rosaries and holy cards and little pieces of palm and I'd feel guilty because sometimes it just all seemed like a joke. If there really is a God don't you think He'd just talk to us once in a while to let us know He is really there?"

"You'd think. But God, as they say, works in mysterious ways."

Going down the stairs to my car, she said, "And then all of a sudden I'd have my faith back. I wouldn't know why it left me and I wouldn't know why it came back. It just would and I didn't have any control over it. Sometimes I think I'm crazy. And I mean clinically."

"That's why my favorite part of the Bible—and the only part that really makes sense to me—is the Book of Job. He asks all the same questions we do. Hey, exactly what's going on down here, anyway? You got little kids dying, you got people killing each other in wars, you've got tycoons letting all these people starve to death. And the best you can come up with is that we have to take it on faith. There's a Graham Greene line about 'the terrible wisdom of God.' I've never been able to figure out if that's a cop-out or the most brilliant thing ever uttered about a deity."

She laughed. "Maybe it's both."

In the car, on the way home, she said, "This is going to be a long haul, Sam."

"I know."

"We'll both naturally want to sleep together. And probably not too long from now, either. But before we do, I'll have to show you where I was operated on. And that'll be difficult for both of us. Maybe most of all for you."

"I can handle it, Linda."

"I hope both of us can handle it, Sam," she said as I pulled up to the curb in front of her house.

I watched her go in and then the feeling of the high school lark faded away utterly. We were past that. She was already an adult and I was being forced by age and circumstance to try and become one, too.

I drove around for an hour before going back to my apartment. I'd always rushed into love before and in ways this time was no different. But there were Linda's complexities to consider.

In some ways it's easier to dazzle women as a lover than it is to be a true friend. I wasn't any Casanova in the sack but I wondered if I was the sensitive guy I liked to imagine myself. She was right. This was going to be tough to handle for both of us.

I knew that tomorrow I'd prepare myself for the night that would eventually come by going to the library and looking up breast cancer. I needed to know a lot more about it. Whenever it was that I finally saw her scars, I wanted to make it as easy as possible for her. For us.

FIFTEEN

RITA SCULLY'S FATHER HAD managed to escape the Knolls by building from scratch a stable that boarded and trained horses. Because he was the only person in the area who had any skill with show horses and jumpers, the gentry—remember here we're talking about the gentry of Black River Falls, not to be confused with the gentry of Greenwich, Connecticut, or Beverly Hills, California—turned his business profitable within a year. The Stables, as it was called, had been in business some twenty years but Bud Scully no longer ran it. He had emphysema so bad, he rarely left his wheelchair. His barn manager was named Cal Rice and he was a good man when sober, which was most of the time; immediately after his benders you could find him forlorn and genuinely ashamed in the church basement where the local AA met seven nights a week.

The meeter and greeter, and the most savvy about show horses and jumpers, was Rita Scully herself. She wore Western even though most of her customers wore riding academy. She sure looked good in an emerald-colored Western shirt with white piping, faded Levis, and black cowboy boots. The shirt set off her green, green eyes and black hair; it set off a couple of other things, too.

I was there at 7 A.M., when she was in the sunlight outside the huge white barn brushing down a colt.

Out on the white-fenced track, a swarthy man walked a pair of huge Palominos. Closer by, a woman with a fierce length of hose was scrubbing out a horse trailer.

When she saw me, Rita said, "That's funny, McCain, I don't remember inviting you to stop out."

"All I'm trying to do is figure out what happened."

"So the judge can show everybody how much smarter she is than Cliffie?"

Like most people in town—like myself, sometimes—she didn't like either Cliffie or the judge.

"No, so we can figure out exactly what happened."

"Exactly what happened," she said, running the brush over the rippling flesh of the sweet, skinny chestnut colt, "is David got drunk and killed himself. It was an accident. He didn't commit suicide, no matter what you might think otherwise."

"There's a third possibility."

"Oh, yeah?" She had a hard beauty but a beauty nonetheless. "Oh, I forgot. You're not only an unsuccessful lawyer, you're also an unsuccessful private eye." From her back pocket she took a currycomb. She set the brush on the ground and started combing him. She'd pause every once in a while to kiss him on the neck. She'd always been sexy, Rita Scully, but I'd never seen her be sweet. There was something touching about the way she'd kissed the horse. She became a new person to me. She was interesting now in a way she'd never been interesting before.

"What if he was murdered?"

And that stopped her. Stopped her from brushing. Stopped her from glancing around the grounds to see that everybody was doing his or her job. In the silence you could hear the horses talking and the birds singing and the sound of a tractor in the fields of a nearby farm. The grass was still silver with dew and even the scent of horseshit had a certain homely sweetness about it.

She said, "Now there's a stupid idea."

"What's so stupid about it?"

"He got drunk and smashed up his car. Case closed." She went back to brushing the horse.

"He talk to you about getting into an argument with anybody recently?"

"He got into arguments all the time. It was just the way he was. That's why Molly was so bad for him. She wanted to change him. Nobody could change David. He was what he was." She glared at me. "And I loved him just the way he was."

"How about Sara Griffin?"

Before she could answer, the woman who'd been hosing out the horse trailer came over and said, "That left tire's bad, Rita. I s'pose we can patch it again but one of these days we're gonna need a new one."

"Well, see what they say at the station. If we can get along without buying a new one, let's do it."

The woman nodded and went back to her trailer. She had a tire jack laid out on the grass and went quickly to work taking the left tire of the trailer off and then transferring it to the back of a battered old Ford pickup.

"So you were saying what, McCain?" She went back to the brush, much longer strokes this time, the colt making satisfied little noises in its throat. She gave it another quick kiss.

"I was starting to ask you about Sara Griffin and Egan."

She wiped sweat from her forehead with back of her hand. "I was waiting him out."

"I'm not following you."

"Waiting for him to grow up a little. See that when it came down to having a wife and kids, I was the one. Not Molly. Not Sara. She gave him status but I gave him love. No matter what happened, he always came back to me."

"Or Molly. Couldn't have been too good for your ego, him seeing all those other girls."

She shrugged. "I got used to it. Anything I've ever really wanted, I've gotten. I lived in the Knolls just long enough to know that when you want something, you have to go through hell to get it. But if you have patience and you don't care what other people think, you'll get it."

"You happen to know where he was Friday night?"

"He didn't kill Sara."

"That's not what I asked you."

She stopped brushing the colt. I reached my hand out and stroked its neck. She was a beauty, a poem of elegant awkwardness and vulnerability.

"He was with one of his tramps. He didn't want to get her into trouble, so he wouldn't say who it was."

The trainer walking the horses on the track called out her name.

"It doesn't matter now anyway, does it, McCain, who he was with? He's dead. Now, I need to get to work. If that's all right with you, I mean."

Jay Norbert was in the can when I got to the DX station. All three bays were in use and the far edge of the drive held four cars waiting to be serviced. Rock and roll blasted from the bays, and on the drive two old-fashioned merchants stood in straw hats and suspenders looking at the remains of Egan's car and shaking their heads.

"Damned Italian food," Norbert said, coming out of the john

about ten minutes after I'd arrived. He had a copy of the local newspaper. "Plays hell with my stomach. I picked up colitis when I worked for Uncle Sam."

We walked out to the tangled remains of David Egan's Merc. Three teenage boys stood there studying it.

"He went right off the edge," one of them said.

"Drunker'n a skunk."

"My brother said he got more ass than a bicycle seat."

Ah, youth.

After Norbert shooed them away, he said, "C'mere a minute."

We walked around to the side of the Merc. The crash had smashed the motor mounts. The engine was tilted so badly it was almost upside down.

He took a long yellow-handled screwdriver out of the back pocket of his uniform and said, "Look at this."

He tapped the hose leading from the brake fluid to the brakes themselves with the tip of his screwdriver.

"You have to look close."

I leaned in, squinted.

"Pretty crude," he said.

"I'll say."

"I figure whoever did it either didn't know anything about cars or tried to make it look like they didn't know anything about cars."

He was right. When you got close enough, it was plain to see the slash in the hose.

"Probably figured that the crash would destroy everything," he said.

"Including the hose."

"So nobody could tell it was cut."

"He couldn't have stopped if he wanted to," I said.

"Yeah, not even if he'd been sober." He took a pack of Marvel cigarettes from his uniform pocket and tamped one out. "I'd offer you one, Sam, but you'd hate me for life. The wife buys these damned things because the A&P always has them on sale." He lit up, coughed. "What'll Cliffie make of this?"

"He won't like it."

He grinned. "That'd sure be too bad, wouldn't it?" Anybody who'd served in the military resented Cliffie because his two uncles on the draft board had managed to keep him from serving. He stared at the car we stood in front of. "This was a hell of a rod. He told me one night that if he took half as good care of all his girlfriends as he did the Merc, he'd probably have a lot happier life."

I nodded to the phone booth. "I'll be back in a few minutes."

I should've been happy about giving Cliffie the bad news, spoiling his neatly resolved case. But I was thinking about Egan. He hadn't exactly been my favorite client, but he'd earned a good share of his anger and bitterness. He'd wanted to improve his lot by using the daughters of the local gentry to prove that he was just as good as everybody else. He'd wanted respect and dignity but he got neither in his death. It was the sort of trashy story— drunken girl-stealing, good-looking kid is murdered in a hick town where he lived with two maiden aunts—that the more lurid of the true detective magazines would buy. Not much respect or dignity there.

When Cliffie came on the line, I said, "You need to get over to the DX station right away."

"What the hell for, Counselor? I'm busy. I can't sit around all day like you."

"Just get the hell over here."

A pause. "You're gonna pay for that, you know. Talkin' to me like that."

"Yeah, well, there're a lot of things I'm gonna have to pay for someday. Just get over here."

The drive got busy. Norbert even had to call one of his mechanics away from his bay to help scrub windows and pump gas. A mechanic can make a station a lot more money than a gas jockey can.

Cliffie made a point of not showing up for half an hour. I sat in the station and listened to tire irons clank on the concrete floor of the service bays and tinny juvenile rock and roll. Frankie Avalon was just never going to replace Chuck Berry on anyplace but Dick Clark's show.

Cliffie came in and said, "Maybe you haven't heard, Counselor, but the little matter with Egan is all wrapped up." He was all khakied up as usual. "He killed Sara and feeling guilty about it killed himself. And if you didn't work for our dear, sweet Judge Whitney, you'd be able to admit I'm right. What'd she put you up to now?"

"Let's go look at the car."

He looked shocked by what he saw. "Crazy sonofabitch. He must've really wanted to die."

"Come over here."

"What for?"

"Look at something."

He sighed and came over. I made the same case Norbert had made to me.

"Oh, no," Cliffie said.

"Oh, no, what? Somebody obviously cut that connection."

"You think I'm gonna fall for this shit?"

"What shit?"

"Somebody cut this, all right. But after the wreck."

"After? Why would somebody do that?"

"Mischief. Some butthole buddies of his decided to have a little fun with me so they cut the line to make it look good."

I saw Norbert and waved him over.

"Morning, Chief," he said when he reached us. "I'm kinda busy, Sam. What can I do for you?"

"He thinks the brake fluid line was cut while the car was sitting here on your drive. I just thought maybe you could clue him in."

"The hell of it is, Sam, I can't."

"What?"

"I can't say exactly when it was cut. You could get the state crime lab to check it out for you, I suppose. If I had to bet that the line was cut before the wreck, that's how I'd bet. But I can't prove it. Sorry."

"The state crime lab," Cliffie said, "couldn't find their ass with both hands."

"I'm requesting that you call them in."

Cliffie smirked at Norbert. "See how free he is with taxpayers' money? Good ole McCain, the taxpayers' friend." He smiled at me. "I'll take it under consideration, as you legal types like to say, Counselor. But I wouldn't hold my breath. I'm a busy man and those fancy-pants crime-lab boys don't like drivin' over here for something like this."

"This is very important," I said.

"Sez you. Me, I say this case is wrapped up. Them two old ladies who raised him don't want people to think he killed himself, so they put a bee in your bonnet about proving it was murder. And that judge of yours figures this is another way to try and humiliate me. All of which adds up to exactly jack shit as far as I'm concerned." He nodded to the gas station. "Norbert, I need to use your crapper."

And that, as far as the khaki-clad, crapper-needing chief of police was concerned, was that.

SIXTEEN

JUST BEFORE NOON, I stopped by the courthouse to talk to the judge. She was in a conference. As I was walking out the back door to where I'd parked my ragtop, I fell into step next to Jack Coyle. He never looked nattier than when he was in his hand-tailored blue suit.

He carried a briefcase and a scowl. "Your friend Judge Whitney gave me one hell of a headache this morning. I'm handling a property matter for a Des Moines firm and need a little more time to prepare myself. She denied it."

"You should never go up against her on Monday mornings. Or Tuesday mornings, come to think of it. Or—" But I stopped joking because he wasn't smiling.

"Now, Jean wants to move, too."

"Move?" I said.

"Build a new house. And in the meantime rent one. She's into a lot of supernatural things. I think it's all crazy but of course I don't want to hurt her feelings."

"Sara Griffin haunting your place, you mean?"

"Not haunting precisely. But something like that. I mean, I'm kind of uneasy being there myself. My God, a dead girl—"

"I still don't understand that part of it."

"What part of it?"

We were now outside in the parking lot. A mix of people came and went as we stood there talking. Dotted everywhere were pairs of other lawyers talking.

"If Egan did kill Sara, why did he leave her in your gazebo? I don't get the connection."

"I don't, either. But he must've been psychotic. He killed her, after all. Maybe he was driving around with the body in his car and—"

I said, "Did you know her?"

"Sure. She was a damned sweet kid. She had her troubles but she was sweet."

He made a point of meeting my eye when he said it, a courtroom trick. You can't tell a lie when you're looking somebody in the eye, can you? Sure. Good liars can, and do, all the time.

"Your daughter knew her, I understand."

"They were friends."

"Sara spend much time around your house?"

This time when he stared at me, there was a suggestion of anger in his All-American blue eyes. "Are you trying to get at something here, Sam?"

"Just trying to understand why the killer would put the body in your gazebo."

He set his briefcase down, pulled out a package of Viceroys from his suit jacket pocket and lit up with a nice, small, silver Ronson lighter. He didn't offer me a smoke.

"So you've heard the stories."

"Not plural. Singular. Story."

"I gave her some tennis lessons. Her psychiatrist told her that exercise would help her with her mood. Exercise, that whole bit. She didn't have any special interest in tennis." He smiled. "She just thought the women in their tennis whites looked very nice. She was a nice-looking girl. And I'm not exactly an old fart. I've been known to get an erection once in a while. All the guys at the country club followed her around like horny dogs. I suppose I felt some manly pride in spending so much time with her. But nothing happened. The stories are bullshit."

"Meaning you'd have no idea why somebody would put her body in your gazebo?"

This smile was malicious. "I swear to God, Sam, working for the judge is starting to poison your mind. You were a nice, clean-cut, sensible young man when you hung out your shingle. I'm sorry to see you're becoming such a paranoid. I love Esme—she's a good friend of ours—but for once I think Cliffie's right. David Egan killed Sara and then felt so guilty about it he killed himself."

"Makes everything tidy, anyway."

He leaned down and picked up his briefcase. "Jean and I like you, too, Sam. I wouldn't want anything to happen to our friendship."

"Egan didn't kill her and he didn't commit suicide."

He shook his head. "Maybe Egan didn't commit suicide, Sam, but you may not want to start bothering people who knew Sara. They're not lowlives. They don't allow themselves to be pushed around."

"Unlike the people who come from the Knolls and get pushed around because they don't have any other choice."

"You think you'll ever get over that class anger of yours, Sam?"

"I doubt it."

He dropped his cigarette to the pavement and twisted his foot on it so it shredded into torn white paper with brown tobacco spilling out. "You're one of us now, Sam. You grew up in the Knolls but that doesn't mean you have to live there the rest of your life—physically or mentally, either one. You don't want to ruin your chances by making a lot of important people mad. And I'm saying this as a friend."

To prove it he put a fatherly hand on my shoulder. "You take care of yourself, Sam. I'm hoping you're going to be a member of our club sometime in the not-too-distant future. You'd be a real asset. And I'd be happy to talk you up to the board. I really would."

A minute later, his bronze Buick came to smooth and powerful life, and he backed out of the lot, his briefcase on the seat next to him, as if it were a passenger.

The Griffin house was built inside a large tract of timber. You got the sense they were hiding from something, the way the hardwoods and pines enveloped their home of native stone and glass and wood—homage, I expect, to Frank Lloyd Wright. There was even a trickle-small Wrightian waterfall behind the long, angular house.

I counted six cars in the drive. All new, all expensive. The Caddy was the most imposing, all white and chrome and sweeping fin. But then Dix Griffin owned the Cadillac dealership.

Mandy Griffin answered my knock. She was a tall, prim woman in a black sheath dress, her graying hair in a chignon. She had good facial bones, an older's woman neck, and blue eyes that didn't look happy to see me at all. "This isn't a good day, McCain."

"I realize that but I just wondered—"

"We know what you're doing and we don't approve."

"What I'm doing?"

"Trying to prove that David Egan didn't kill our daughter. Of course he did."

Dix was in the door then. As a longtime car dealer, he couldn't find it in himself to be rude to anybody. After all, he wouldn't want to kill a potential sale.

"Oh, now, honey," he said, "McCain's just doing what that damned Esme Whitney wants him to do. He wouldn't be doing this on his own so there's no reason to take it personally."

He was big, he was hammy, he spoke in a Southern dialect that seemed contrived. He always spoke of his Southern boyhood but he'd lived up here for forty years. The reverse of your friend who goes on a four-day trip to London and comes back with a British accent.

He wore a black suit with a white shirt and dark blue tie. But the shirt collar was open and the knot of his tie rode at his sternum. His fleshy face was boozy red and he was sweaty. He looked as if he were at an event that combined mourning with poker. Hard to believe he was a Yale man—old Southern money—but then William Buckley Jr. got through there so I suppose anything is possible.

"Cliff called just a few minutes ago and told us what you were up to, McCain, and I have to tell you, we agree with him. Egan killed her, all right, and then he killed himself. I'll give him that much, anyway. He had that much good in him—to realize what he'd done and make his peace with the Lord."

"Somebody cut his brake line."

"Cliff said you'd say that, too. He said, near as he can tell, somebody cut it after Egan's car sat out all night."

"You're a terrible little man," Mandy said, "and I want you to get into your car and drive away right now."

Her voice was loud enough that their other guests started peeking out the front window to get a look at me. Most of them, recognizing me, frowned. Difficult as it is to imagine, I am not a universally beloved figure.

"Don't you want to know who really killed your daughter, Mrs. Griffin?"

"We do know, McCain," Griffin said, sliding his arm around his wife's frail shoulder. "We're not going to waste our time—and our feelings—on some damned stupid contest between Esme and Chief Sykes. He's made his share of mistakes in the past, that's true, but he also happens to be right on this one. And that's all we have to say on the subject."

He closed the door. His guests were lined up in the front window like kids forced to stay inside on a rainy day. I was like an exciting TV show, the way they watched me get in my ragtop, U-turn on the drive, and head back to the front gates. Fascinating stuff.

I called Linda at the hospital in Iowa City.

"So you just called? Just to say hi? That's very nice of you. In fact, I was thinking that maybe you'd like to get a pizza tonight. My treat, Sam."

"That sounds great. I'll pick you up at seven."

"Just remember—"

"I remember. We're going easy. And that's fine with me."

"This will get to be a real drag for you someday, Sam. I'm sorry."

"I'm not sorry at all. I like being with you and that's all we need to say."

"Thanks, Sam. See you at seven."

The librarian gave me a curious look when I asked her where I might find a book on cancer. Having been a librarian here since I was a kid, she was naturally concerned that my reading wasn't for my mom or dad.

"Everything all right at home, Sam?"

"Everything's fine, Mrs. Anderson."

She was the only librarian who'd bought both Edgar Rice

Burroughs and Robert Heinlien for the library in those long-ago days after the war when the country was on one of its sporadic improve-your-mind campaigns, which always meant promoting the sort of books kids didn't want to read. A few libraries were forced to give away all their Burroughs books. She'd shown up at the graduation ceremony for the law school and given me a nice auntly kiss on the cheek as I passed down the aisle clutching my diploma. You don't forget people like that.

I was pretty self-conscious about it. When I found the book she suggested, I took it to a corner table and kind of hunched over the book.

I wasn't shocked. I sort of knew what I was going to see. It made me mad looking at the woman whose torso they'd color-photographed. The healthy breast next to the flat line of scar next to it. I thought of Linda and then of my mom and then of my kid sister. I wanted to hold somebody responsible for this. But mad became sad and I thought of my aunt Barb, who'd died of it, and the lady down the street who was fighting it and all of a sudden it seemed overwhelming, like every woman in the world was going to get it eventually. I closed the book. I wanted a cigarette, speaking of cancer. I sat there and thought of Linda and what this must mean to her. And how she had to live in daily fear that it would come back. Some little routine test, some little sign, and then your doctor was talking about surgery again; or worse, *not* talking about surgery because it was too late even for that. I still wanted somebody to blame for all this. Random cosmic bad luck wasn't good enough. I needed to see a WANTED poster with some bastard's face and name on it.

The cigarette tasted so good, I had two of them, just sitting in my ragtop in the warm, glowing autumn afternoon watching the old guys play checkers on the bird-bombed green park benches. I wanted Linda with me. A healthy, long-lived Linda. Hard to imagine the darkness of death when I thought of her on so fetching a day.

The judge would be wanting to hear from me, and since I had nothing much to report I thought that maybe it was time I visit Brenda Carlyle, which I'd been putting off. Her husband, Mike, had gotten all the way to Chicago in the Golden Gloves just before he left for Korea. He worked at his old man's lumberyard and spent his idle hours beating the crap out of any guy who so much as glanced at his wife, which wasn't easy not to do, believe me, her being one of the most quietly erotic women ever born in our little valley here. She is not innocent of her charms. In high school, I'm told, she used to pursue various boys and, when done with them, turn them over to Mike for summary punishment. Mike either didn't know that she'd approached the boys, rather than the other way around, or he chose not to know.

Certain legends were passed among the panting young men in our town. Many of them concerned Brenda. Most of the stories were variations on the stuff the panting young men had read in the sort of books Kenny Chesmore writes. You know, that she liked to stand on certain husband-gone nights draped only in the gauziest of teddy-bear nighties and try to lure foolish boys inside in the way a sea siren would. That she rewarded the best high school football player of the year with a special night all their own. And that at Christmastime she gave herself to the young man who struck her as the most exciting.

But remember, folks, this is Black River Falls, after all, and there isn't much else to do but think up stories like these.

I decided to stop by the lumberyard and make sure that Mike was at work. Didn't want him to surprise me by opening the door of his home.

The lumberyard always unmanned me. I come from a long line

of handymen. If a tornado knocks your house down tonight, my dad and a couple of his brothers will have it standing, good as new, twenty-four hours later. I have trouble pounding nails in straight. Or getting screws to stay in. And anything I painted always came out striped, as if I'd used several subtly different colors. When I was in tenth grade my dad asked me to help him install a new window over the kitchen sink. We got the window in all right, but when I was putting the shutter back on, my hammer accidentally slammed a corner of it and shattered glass all over my mom, who was innocently washing dishes. My dad never asked me to help him again and I couldn't blame him.

But the lumberyard dazzled me with all its manly secrets and rites of passage: whine of electric saw, smell of fresh cut lumber, stacks of wood in the yard, men in big overalls, their pipes tucked into the corners of their mouths as they loaded lumber into the backs of their trucks, their tool belts packed with all sorts of arcane instruments that would be lost on me. I had a pair of bib overalls but the legs were too long. And I had some tools but Mrs. Goldman kept them because she used them—and used them well—much better than I did.

I saw him and he saw me. He didn't like me. One night in a bar his wife had grabbed me and swung me out onto the dance floor. It was fast dancing but he still hadn't liked it. He had a good memory. He'd been glowering at me ever since that night. And that had been at least four years ago.

He didn't wear overalls. He wore a shirt and tie and trousers. He was huge but quick and deft for his size. He picked up a pile of two-by-fours and dropped them in the bed of a truck.

No reason to stay there. I turned and walked away, inhaling the perfume of fresh sawn lumber.

I got in my ragtop and drove maybe three blocks to the narrow road that would take me to the Carlyle house when I decided I'd better check in at my office.

"Uh, just a minute, okay?" Jamie answered.

This is one I hadn't heard before. I'd heard "It's your nickel," I'd heard "Uh, Mr. C's office."

Now she said: "Damn, I just spilled my nail polish all over the desk."

There was no sense being angry. God was punishing me for all my sins.

"Okay, I'm back," she said.

"It's me."

"Oh, gosh Mr. C, I've been trying to find you."

"You have?"

"Well, I was about to try and find you I guess I should say. Turk brought me a sandwich and we're just sort of eating it."

A lurid picture of them humping on my desk filled the drive-in screen of my mind.

"Ah, lunch."

"She tried to kill herself, Mr. C."

"Who did?"

"Molly."

"Molly Blessing?"

"Yeah. Molly Blessing. Her mom called and said Molly wants to talk to you."

"Where is she now?"

"The hospital. Not the Catholic one."

That was how she always referred to things. The Catholic one or not the Catholic one. The dime store that's not Woolworth's. The pizza joint that's not out on Highway 6.

"I'm going over there now. Were there any other messages?"

She cupped the phone. "Didn't somebody else call, Turk?"

A muffled male voice.

"Turk says no other calls. I was in the ladies room for a while, Mr. C. He was watching the phone."

Watching I wouldn't mind. Talking into it I would. If her phone mannerisms were bad, imagine Turk's. He's Irish by the way. God only knows where the name Turk came from.

I drove straight to the hospital. Not the Catholic one.

I wasn't surprised by a suicide attempt, not after the way she'd acted the other night.

When I got to her room, the nurse said, "Her parents are downstairs talking to the doctor. You can have five minutes or so. She's weak." BETTY BYRNES read her name tag.

"What happened?"

"She got into her mother's tranquilizers. Took a dozen or so. Fortunately, they're not especially strong dosage-wise. She'll be fine."

She didn't look fine. The only vibrant color in the room was her coppery hair. Everything else was white, including her face. She looked like a dying angel. She seemed to be sleeping. I didn't want to wake her up. I started to turn and walk away.

"Hi, Sam."

I turned back to her. "Hi, Molly."

"Pretty stupid thing to do, huh?"

"Yeah," I said, walking over to her. "Pretty stupid."

Deep sigh. There was a table on wheels next to her bed. A silver metal water pitcher was beaded with sweat. An abridged version of the King James Bible. A movie magazine with Rock Hudson on it.

She said, "I just couldn't deal with it. It really hit me. You know, that he was dead and not coming back. I had a couple of drinks from my father's bar in the basement and then I found my mom's tranquilizers. I don't remember much after that."

"You in any pain?"

"Not really. Just kind of groggy. This was so dumb. It's embarrassing."

"Anything I can get you?"

She tried to smile. "A phone call from David would be nice." Then, "I wish I were as strong as Rita."

"She's pretty tough."

"She wouldn't pull a stunt like this one." She laid her head back. Closed her eyes. "You think I'll ever get over it, Sam?"

"I don't know about getting over it. But you'll be able to deal with it."

"I wish I were an adult."

"We all wish we were adults."

She opened one eye and smiled at me. "You've got a great sense of humor." Then, "David did, too. He was never boring to be with. Never. You could just sit somewhere and he could keep you entertained for hours. I'd never known anybody like that before." Then, "My folks told me Cliffie's mad at you because you've been asking people a lot of questions."

"Just trying to make sure that Egan's death was accidental."

"You didn't like him much, did you, Sam?"

"Sometimes I did. Sometimes he was pretty hard to take. The way he felt sorry for himself and everything."

"He had good reasons to feel sorry for himself, Sam."

This wasn't the time for a debate. "His aunts will see to it that he gets a nice funeral."

"I may still be in here."

The nurse came in. "Her folks'll be back in a few minutes." She had a kind, middle-aged face. She gazed down at Molly. "She conned me into phoning your office and inviting you up here. But I'd just as soon the doctor doesn't know I did it."

"I really appreciate you coming here, Sam."

"I just wanted to make sure you were all right."

The nurse beamed. "She'll be fine. All her vitals are good and she's in much better spirits this morning than she was last night."

"What I am mostly is embarrassed," said Molly. "'Poor, pathetic Molly crying out for help again.' I can just hear people saying that now."

I leaned over and kissed her on the forehead. She took my hand and squeezed it.

In the hall, Betty said, "She's a nice kid. But unlucky."

"Unlucky how?"

"David Egan. My oldest daughter went out with him a few times. I know you were his lawyer, Mr. McCain. And maybe he was your friend. But mothers aren't thrilled when their daughter takes up with somebody like him. They're like professional heart-breakers, boys like him. They want to wound the girl in some way and walk away. Fortunately for my daughter, she recognized this in him pretty early. She made sure he didn't hurt her. She finally met a nice kid and told David good-bye. I was on my knees a whole lot of nights praying that Doris wouldn't fall in love with him." She nodded to the room. "Poor little Molly wasn't so lucky."

The elevator doors started to open.

"I think I'll take the stairs," I said.

"I don't blame you," Betty said. "Her parents are in a mood to tear into somebody. And I'd hate to see it be you."

SEVENTEEN

I HAD TO PASS THE Kelly house on my way out of town so I decided to see if they were home and if they would let me spend a little time in David's room. I doubted if Cliffie had even bothered checking it out. Since he was convinced he knew what had happened, why would he? I'd have to check the lumberyard again to make sure Mike was there. Might as well get this done first.

I parked in the drive and heard them talking in the backyard. They were hanging white sheets on the clothesline. A wind was filling the dried sheets at the far end of the line and flapping them in the wind like the sails of pirate ships. Newly mown grass smelled fresh and crisp; and on a small stone cookout grill—one I suspected that David had made—a couple of burgers were cooking. On the edge of a picnic table you could see catsup, mustard, relish, and a stack of paper plates.

Amy had just stuck a wooden clothespin in her mouth when I approached. I heard Emma but I couldn't see her. "I'm washing our special tablecloth. Emma's birthday's coming up."

"She's a year and a half older than I am, Sam," Emma said, working her way out from behind a sheet.

"Year and a quarter," Amy said.

It was the easy jocularity of two women who had literally spent their entire lives together. I'd read an article about how close companions could virtually become one person after so many years. I believed it.

"I wondered if I could look around David's room."

The look that passed between them surprised me. Good old Sam suddenly became good old Sam the intruder.

"Now why on earth would you want to do that, Sam?" Amy said.

Now I was more than surprised. I was suspicious myself. Pretty harmless request.

"Well, you hired me to find out what happened to him. I just thought that maybe I'd turn up something in his room."

The look again.

"Well," Emma said. "Wish you would've given us a little warning is all."

"Yes," Amy said, "we did the best we could but it wasn't easy to keep things picked up."

"We just don't want you thinking we're bad housekeepers, Sam."

I wondered what they didn't want me to find. What was there to be so secretive about? Especially in light of the fact that I was working for them. Supposedly, anyway.

"Maybe you could stop back later this afternoon, Sam," Emma said. "Give us a chance to pick things up first."

I glanced from one to the other. Such sweet old ladies. Such a sweet old day. Scent of laundry and fresh cut grass. And even a monarch butterfly perched on one end of the clothesline.

And yet there was something a little sinister about these two old ladies now. Norman Rockwell's first drive-in movie poster—two sweet-faced little old ladies who were actually in

the vanguard of an alien race about to take over planet earth. I
half expected to see killer rays shooting from their eyes.

"You know," I said, "if I didn't know better, I'd say you two
had something to hide."

Amy was the blusher of the two. Her cheeks hued crimson at
my words and her gaze fell to the grass.

Emma burst out with a rich but fake laugh. "Well, he's found
us out, Amy. About our criminal past."

Amy wasn't as good at faking. She managed to stammer
through, "Uh, oh yes, our past—criminal—past."

"How about around suppertime?" I said.

"Now that would be fine, Sam," Emma said, keeping her fake
enthusiasm up. "We really aren't trying to hide anything. We just
want to pick things up a little."

They stood there smiling at me. Amy had her hands behind her
back. Maybe she was holding a blood-dripping ax—

Another drive-in movie poster.

I decided to try the office again. This time Jamie answered right
away and in English. "Law office."

"Any calls?"

All this came out in a gush: "Gosh, you know who called you, Mr.
C? Andrea Prescott. Just about the most stuck-up girl who ever
went to our high school. She was a good friend of Sara Griffin's. She
said she has to talk to you right away. She called from Iowa City.
She's going to school there. She said she'll be back here in about half
an hour and wants you to meet her at the Indian mounds."

"She say why she wants to talk to me?"

"No. She was her usual snotty self."

Jamie was never sweeter than when she felt snubbed. She was
little-kid hurt, right up front, all naked pain. She didn't try to
hide it for the sake of saving face.

"I'm sorry, Jamie."

"Oh, it's all right, Mr. C. I didn't cry or nothin'."

"Good. I'll talk to you in a while, all right?"

Once again, I had to postpone my trip to see Brenda Carlyle.

In ninth grade I had to write a paper on the mound builders. These Indians were descended in some way we still don't understand from tribes that thousands of years earlier killed huge bison by running them over cliffs or running them into bogs, where they were trapped. The Indians then speared them to death. Bows and arrows hadn't been invented yet. Spears alone wouldn't kill the animals but cunning would. And the forbears of the mound builders seemed to have plenty of that. Running twelve-hundred-pound animals off a cliff is a pretty bright idea.

Except for certain stone artifacts, we don't really know much about these ancient hunters except that they practiced communal living. Bison of the size they hunted meant a thousand pounds of meat and that would presumably have fed everybody in the tribe for some time.

We know a lot more about the mound builders who came after them, though these people, too, remain mysterious. The mounds are large, above-ground tombs of maybe one hundred and fifty feet in length and maybe three feet in height. When they were opened, scientists found evidence of a people who were far more sophisticated than any who came before and many who came after. It was as if this certain people took a quantum leap up the ladder of knowledge. But then a strange quirk occurs. The native peoples that European explorers first met do not seem to have descended from the mysterious mound builders. The later people did not have the skills or scientific understanding of the builders of the mounds.

So who were the mound builders and what were they all

about? I'm waiting for God to tell me. Apparently He's the only one who knows for sure.

Or maybe Andrea Prescott knew. She was a cold blond, who was not quite as good-looking as she thought, all done up in several hundred dollars of good clothes—blue suede car coat, dark blue sweater, light blue slacks—and a pair of sunglasses that gave her the faint air of a starlet. She had set her very nice bottom on the edge of a picnic table and was in the process of lighting a cigarette when I walked up to her.

"God, you really *are* short."

"Why, thank you."

"I suppose that came off a little shitty." She put out a limp slender hand. I half expected she half expected me to kiss it. I gave it a good shaking. "You can do better than that, McCain. Put a little hurt into it." She smiled. She apparently found this all terribly, terribly amusing. *Dear, dear Noel.* She said, "Did anybody warn you about me?"

"Just that pest control company."

"My mother says I'm a bitch on wheels. But I really don't mean to be."

"My faith in humanity has been restored at last."

I wanted a peek at her eyes. The shades made that impossible. "You're a sarcastic little shit."

"Thank you again."

She took a terminal drag on her smoke, exhaled, and said, "I'm the one who called you the other night."

"'It wasn't an accident'—that thing?"

"Yes. I thought I was pretty good."

"Not bad."

"Because it wasn't, you know." She reached into the pocket of her car coat and withdrew one of those tiny bottles of liquor they serve on airliners. She had herself a pop then returned bottle to pocket. "Sara was my cousin."

"Lucky girl."

"She said somebody was after her."

"Did she say who?"

"She wasn't sure. She just had this sense. She was sort of a goody-two-shoes. She had no imagination at all. I used to put her on all the time and she always took everything I said seriously. A total square. That's why I believed her. If my little cousin thought somebody was after her, then they were." She walked over to the mounds. "You know anything about these things?"

"Not much except that the people who built them were way ahead of their time."

She sighed. "I decided to go to Iowa instead of Northwestern so I could be closer to this boy I'm kind of in love with, who pledged Greek at the university. God, I wonder if it was worth it. I wanted to study real things. Not a bunch of Indians, for God's sake."

"The university's a good school."

"You went there, I suppose?"

"Yeah, after a couple of years Oxford started to get boring so I came back here."

"Did I ever tell you how much I hate patter? Don, that's my fiancé, people think he's stupid because he can't small-talk. I think it's a sign of intelligence, not being a smart mouth all the time."

"Like certain short private investigators you could name?"

She took off her glasses. She had wondrous beautiful blue eyes. "Exactly." Then, "You wouldn't know anything about these Indians would you?"

"They're dead."

"Patter."

"Actually, they're very interesting. There's a book on them at the library downtown."

"Did they ever have to fight dinosaurs?"

"Different time period."

"Oh." She was disappointed but then most people are disappointed when they find out dinosaurs weren't involved.

"I'm in a hurry, Andrea. What did you want to tell me?"

She smoked her cigarette right down to the nub. "The time she had her breakdown? It was because she was seeing an older man."

"I kind of figured that."

"She was a sophomore."

"I know."

"In high school."

"I know."

"Seeing this forty-five-year-old."

"Are you going to tell me his name?"

"I'll bet you already know his name."

"I'm betting Jack Coyle."

She smiled. "You're not half as dumb as you look."

I laughed. "You know, if you were a real bitch you wouldn't have to work so hard at it. You work up a sweat about it and that's never any good. Instead of bitchy, you just come off sort of sad. Maybe even a little pathetic. Maybe you didn't get the Christmas present you wanted one year. Or maybe your daddy would never kiss you. Or maybe you weren't potty trained properly."

"Try walking in on my mom screwing my uncle's brains out."

"Oh. I guess I was wrong. Sorry." It was a pretty dramatic moment. A thing like that could turn anybody into a bitch. "When did it happen?"

"It didn't really happen. I just wanted to see if I could get you to feel sorry for me for a half a minute. You should've seen your face when I told you the bit about my uncle."

"So your mom didn't sleep with him?"

"His own *wife* won't sleep with him. He's got this skin condition all over his body."

"Ah."

She smirked. "You should've seen your face, McCain."

I knew my face was red. She was some piece of work. "So had she heard from Jack Coyle lately?"

"Three times in one week. Wanting to get together."

"So that's what you meant by it wasn't an accident?"

"He has a terrible temper. She told me that much. I could see him killing her and David."

I pictured him in his tennis whites. I guessed I could see him killing them, too.

"He was completely obsessed with her," she said. "Say, you wouldn't write a paper for me, would you?"

"Too busy."

"A hundred dollars?"

"Too busy."

A smirk. "A hundred dollars and an hour with me in the back seat."

I decided to surprise her. "You know something?"

"What?"

"I like you."

"Sure you do."

"I do. You're as insecure as I am but you don't handle it well at all. You need to relax. The bitch acts gets old fast."

"I got you going, didn't I? With that story about my mom and my uncle?"

"Yes, you did. I felt sorry for you. I could actually see you as a little girl walking into that bedroom. What you must've seen and how you must've felt." I reached out and shook her hand. "Thanks for the lead on Jack Coyle. It may come in handy."

After finishing our handshake, I started toward my car.

She said, to my back, "McCain?"

"Yeah?" I kept on moving.

"What I told you about walking in on my mom was true."

"I kind of figured it was." And I had.

"That's why they got a divorce. But she wasn't with my uncle." Beat for maximum dramatic effect: "She was with my aunt."

EIGHTEEN

MIKE CARLYLE MADE IT easy for me. He stood in the entrance to his lumberyard talking to a customer. He glanced at my ragtop as I drove by but didn't seem to find it interesting enough to glance for long.

As I drove out to his place, I noticed all the early spooks appearing all over town, jack o'lanterns and cardboard witches in windows, and a few scarecrows on front lawns. Halloween. With the smoky scent of autumn on the air, it made you want to be a kid again when the most frightening thing you had to face was boogeymen you could buy at Woolworth's. I thought of Linda. A cancer ward was about as scary a thing as I could imagine.

The Carlyle house was one of those new ranch styles that sprawled over half an acre in a valley. The wine-colored house was surrounded by jack pines that hid it almost completely when you approached, as I did, from the west. A long metal rail ran in front of the place up on the roadside to keep cars from sailing off the asphalt and smashing into the house below.

I found a small park a quarter mile away and walked back. I didn't want to advertise I was coming so she'd have time to hide.

The sun was just beginning to set. A yellow school bus roared past, scattering dust and gravel. The air was brisk and clean. I always told big city people that I liked living in a small city because I was so close to the outdoors. But I didn't *get* outdoors all that much.

The drive was a long slope of gravel leading to a two-stall garage with one car in it and a huge water tank. I went past them and on to the house.

No dog. Out here, on the edge of town and on every farm, there's a dog. There are just enough prison breaks, just enough roaming intruders to make a dog a good investment. But there was no dog.

I knocked on a screen door that ricocheted each time I struck it. Nothing. But the car in the garage told me she was in there.

I walked around the house peeking in windows. The furnishings were new but not expensive or noteworthy. Just good solid stuff. There was a cuckoo clock somewhere that celebrated the half hour. Four-thirty.

I went back to the screen door. Tried the front door behind it. Unlocked. I pushed in and called her name several times. There was an interior silence that bothered me, and as I looked around at the furniture, the silence became more pronounced.

I tried to put the size and ferocity of Mike Carlyle out of my mind. Cute little tricks—kicking guys in the balls chief among them—could buy you a few cheap victories from time to time. But not with men like Carlyle. You'd never get close enough to kick him.

I decided an inspection was required and I decided that it was best if I could pull it off in less than .0000038 seconds.

I went room to room and found nothing other than the same good solid unremarkable furnishings I'd found in the living room. The bedroom wall was interesting. Several framed photos of Brenda in various bikinis over a span of several years. Kind of a grotto to one sexy body. She'd put on weight at about mid-point in the span of pictures but it was the kind of weight that somehow only enhanced her sexuality. I got a pleasant little ache in my groin looking at the later ones. Mike was nowhere to be found in the photos.

I found her in the john and even though she was naked I didn't get any little ache in my groin, pleasant or otherwise.

She'd been taking a bath when somebody had struck her on the side of the skull, much as Sara Griffin had been struck. The bath water was filthy with her blood and the pink-tiled bathroom stank of her dying and her death. Her left hand, resting on the edge of the bathtub's side, was crabbed into a claw. Her green eyes glared up at me. A tiny trickle of blood had wormed its way from her nostril to her upper lip.

You could see the wide swaths of dried soap and water on the sink, walls, doorknob. The place had been wiped down thoroughly.

I haven't seen that many corpses in my young life but I'll tell you one thing, that old Irish maxim is true. When you see a dead person, one of your first thoughts is how you'll look when *you're* dead. There's your mortality staring right up at you.

After that moment passed, I realized two things. I needed a cig-arette and I needed to get out of this house.

As I got to the end of the hall, a heavy vehicle popped gravel and came to a rumbling stop somewhere near the front door. Mike and the big Chevrolet pickup he drove for the lumberyard. I was sure of it. I went to the curtained front window, peeked out. He had just left the truck, toting a large cardboard box in both hands.

I had some alternatives. I could hide, I could run, or I could confront him.

Just as the front door was shoved inward, I thought of a fourth alternative. There was a black telephone sitting on a dry bar. I picked up the receiver and dialed the police station.

Mike Carlyle saw me just as Mooney, the asthmatic man who answers the phone in the daytime, wheezed, "Police station."

"Mooney, this is Sam McCain. Tell the chief that I just found Brenda Carlyle dead in her bathtub. He'd better get out here fast."

Carlyle dropped the heavy box on the floor and made a sound deep in his throat that combined shock and rage and loss. The noise paralyzed me, forced me for the first time to see him as a human being, the eloquence of his stunned pain.

Then he came rushing at me.

PART 3

NINETEEN

His shoulder collided with mine. He was big enough and crazed enough to knock me several feet across the living room without even being conscious of it.

He was on his way to the bathroom and to his wife. I'd expected violence from him, verbal and physical. *What was I doing here? Had I been sleeping with her? Why I had I killed her?*

He didn't walk out of the bathroom. He exploded at me, this gigantic crazed animal ducking his head as if he were going to attack me the way a bull attacks a matador. "You killed her and now I'm gonna kill you!"

"I didn't kill her, Mike. I didn't have any reason to. Now calm down."

I grabbed a fifth of whiskey from the bar and got ready for him. I figured he wouldn't calm down. When he got about two feet from me, I smashed it into the side of his head and stepped aside. And then I decided we were in a Warner Brothers cartoon where the good guy, the extremely psychotic sadist Bugs Bunny, slams somebody over the head with an anvil, only to see the bad guy shrug it off and keep right on charging.

Which is just what happened.

While he grabbed me by the throat, I had time to swipe a fifth of scotch from the bar top. And then he was running with me right back into the wall.

There is nothing good to say about strangling. Somebody can knock you out and do you a favor. You don't have to be awake while they stomp you. But strangling folks takes a relatively long time and you're awake until near the very end.

He'd clamped his hands on me so tight I forgot everything except trying to breathe. Instinctively, though, I knew enough to hold on to the fifth of scotch.

I dangled about two feet off the carpet. He alternated between choking me and slamming my head into the wall. It was hard to tell which I enjoyed more. I kept kicking him in the shins because that's where my toes were. He'd curse when I'd get him a good one but his hands never let up on their pressure.

"You killed her, you bastard. You killed her."

I wasn't in any position to argue, much as I wanted to. Hell, I was a lawyer. I could argue my case.

I don't know how long it was before I started losing consciousness. Couple minutes, maybe. But suddenly I was hot and cold—shivering cold—and I started losing strength and I kept trying to gasp down some air and—

And then I did it. I gathered enough strength and intelligence to raise the scotch bottle and smash the neck of it against the wall behind me.

If he heard the smashing glass, he didn't let on. He just kept pressing my larynx harder. He knew he was almost home.

I stabbed him in the head.

Not all that deep but enough so that there was a lot of blood immediately. Enough so that the pain forced him to drop me and to fall away. Enough so that he tripped backward over the coffee table and sprawled face up on the couch.

"Now listen to me, you big stupid ape," I said, advancing toward him with the smashed bottle. The jagged parts ran with his blood. "I didn't kill your wife. I didn't know your wife. I talked to her once. That's all. And that's all we did was talk. You understand?"

I don't know what I expected. But whatever I expected, it wasn't this awful stretching silence with him looking up at me like a sad lost child. Just this awful stretching silence broken finally by a single sob.

"You really didn't kill her?"

"No, Mike, I really didn't kill her."

"I'm not any big stupid ape."

"No, I don't guess you are."

"There're a lot of smart football players."

He didn't want to think about his dead wife so he led us off the trail. A little diversion.

"There was this fullback who had a doctorate in—"

"Mike."

I looked at him.

"What?"

"Sit up. I'll get you a drink."

"I think you broke all the bottles."

"Just two. Now sit up on the couch and I'll get you a drink."

I got him his drink and he said, "You see her in there?" I set the bottle of sour mash on the coffee table in front of him.

"Yeah. That's why I called the police station."

He finished off the second drink and helped himself to a third. "She was sleeping around on me."

"I'm sorry."

"I never even hit her when I found out." He got up clumsily and stalked over to the drapes and yanked on a cord. A rose-colored, dusk sky filled the room with more melancholy than it could rightly tolerate. "She promised me she'd never fall in love with any of them. And she kept her word."

He put his drink down on the top of the TV cabinet. He put his head in his big hands. He wept.

A couple of times he sounded as if he were going to vomit. A couple of times I had the sense that he was going to let go and start smashing things. A couple of times I forgot myself and felt sorry for him. It's hard to hate somebody when you see that they're not any stronger than you are, and break just as easily.

The sirens sounded lonely in the early nightfall. Most people would be sitting down to the evening meal, Dad home from the factory or the store, Mom serving the food, and the kids ready to bolt as soon as their stomachs were full. Mom and Dad would watch TV and a couple of times during the course of the evening they'd remember why they married each other, those sweet pure remembrances that buttress good marriages, and for those moments they wouldn't be old married folks, they'd be the kids they'd once been, all full of hope and excitement and each other.

I wondered if Mike had ever had nights like that with Brenda. I somehow doubted it. They'd always been reckless people—he loved to fight, to play high-stakes poker, to tell you how much better-looking his wife was than yours—and he'd liked to parade her in front of other men, almost daring them to approach her.

And this is where it all came to an end. You always wonder where and when your own life will end, I guess. But you don't wonder where and when the life of the woman you love will end. Now he knew.

I left him there and went out and heated up the half pot of coffee that was still on the stove.

I was just pouring a cup when the reenactment of World War II began. It sounded that way, anyway. Later on, I counted the emergency vehicles. Six of them. Including Cliffie on his Harley. The way he backed off his pipes I wondered if he was literally trying to wake the dead.

Cliffie allowed the two men who actually knew what they were doing to take over. Their biggest problem was keeping Cliffie from spoiling evidence.

Because Mike was a well-known former jock, we got TV people as well as newspaper and radio ones. Cliffie called one of his press conferences and proceeded to say all sorts of stupid and unprofessional things into several microphones. But he had his khaki uniform and his badge on his person and images of Glenn Ford dancing in his mind, so he was off and flying. If the county attorney, who would have to prosecute this case, was hearing Cliffie he was probably considering suicide.

The crowd came soon after. There must be people who drive around at night looking for accidents and tragedies. They're just there, suddenly, vampires who live not on blood but on the misery of others. This was a remote area and yet here they were. They know enough to speak discreetly, they know enough not to interfere with the police activities, and they know enough to move here or there when the officials ask them. They don't want to jeopardize their feeding.

I saw a doctor give Mike an injection that I assume was a sedative; I saw Mike's lawyer walk through the front door; and I saw a man from the county attorney's office trying not to smirk while Cliffie shouted various theories at him. They were standing out on the front lawn, off to the side, isolated from the vampires and the press.

I was just about to leave when Cliffie roped me into the conversation with Jim McGuire, a very lowly lawyer in the county attorney's little fiefdom.

McGuire was scrawny and dressed himself as I often did in

suits from the Paris Men's Shop available only at Sears Roebuck. He had blue eyes, red lips, and pipe-smoker yellow teeth.

Cliffie said, "Here's a guy who can back me up. Tell him, Counselor. You know, about how she slept around."

I said, "She slept around."

"A lot of women sleep around," McGuire said.

"In this town?" Cliffie sounded shocked.

"Yes," McGuire said, winking at me, "in this very town, Chief."

But Cliffie was always good on his feet. "Yeah, well, maybe so, but how many of them got themselves murdered this afternoon?"

"With a mind like that, Chief," McGuire said, "you should've been a trial lawyer."

Cliffie caught the sarcasm. "Sure, and let killers go free the way McCain here does?" Then, "You know anybody she was sleeping with, McCain?"

"I don't know this for a fact. But I think David Egan was one of them. I know for sure he spent time with her. I can't say positively that he slept with her."

"He slept with everybody," Cliffie said. "But he's dead, so we can eliminate him for this."

"Good point," McGuire said. "Being dead is about the best alibi you can have."

"I'm gonna tell your boss what a wise guy you are," Cliffie said. "So knock it off."

McGuire knew that he'd reached Cliffie's invisible line in the sand. He said, "This is my first murder, Chief. I'm just trying to sound tough by making jokes. I didn't mean to offend you."

Cliffie slid his arm around McGuire's shoulder. "See how nice he talks when he wants to, Counselor? Maybe you could take lessons from him."

"How much you charge an hour for lessons, McGuire?" I said.

But he knew better than to join in the fun. "I think I'll go see how the investigation is going. Thanks, Chief."

We watched him go and Cliffie said, "I've got Mike's ass nailed on this one. Too bad, too, because he's one hell of a nice guy."

"Mike didn't do it."

"What the hell's that supposed to mean?"

"I was here before he got home."

"Maybe he came here earlier, killed her, went back to work and then drove back here and pretended to be out of his mind when he found her. You were here so he put on a little show for you."

"Whoever killed Sara Griffin and Egan killed Brenda."

He made a face. "That sounds like the judge talking."

"That's me talking. First of all, Mike'll have an alibi. He was at work all afternoon. And second of all, she was with Egan the night you had him killing Sara Griffin."

"That was the alibi he wouldn't tell us about? Brenda?"

"That's right."

"Hell, no wonder he wouldn't talk. Mike would've killed him." He shrugged. "So Mike found out about Egan and he killed her. Simple as that, Counselor. It all ties together—Sara Griffin causes Egan to commit suicide; Mike finds out Brenda was shacking up with Egan and he kills her. A dope could figure that one out."

And a dope just has, I wanted to say. But Cliffie'd had enough abuse for today.

"If you say so, Chief," I said.

Somebody called for him from the front door of the house.

I walked back to my car and headed back to town.

On the dance floor, she said, "You smell good."

"New aftershave."

"Oh."

"You smell good, too."

She smiled nervously. "Same old perfume."

"But it's a good one."

"I'm glad you like it."

You know how it goes when you're both thinking about one thing—in this case how far we'd go tonight—while you're talking about something else.

So far tonight, over pizza and three mild drinks each, we'd talked about Cliffie pestering her for more information, her mom wanting to get a dog, her sister in Indianapolis worried that her husband was having an affair, how she was able to smell winter on the air this afternoon, how most people never believed her when she said she could smell winter, and how there was a new intern at the hospital who wasn't so hot at washing his hands and how a couple of the nurses had decided to say something to one of the staff doctors about the matter.

As the music ended, she said, "You mind if we sit down?"

The restaurant was small, dark, and filled with people who seemed to be quite earnest about having a good time. There was a lot of empty laughter and a lot of drunken kidding with the waitresses and a lot of middle-aged dry-humping on the dance floor whenever a ballad was played.

She said, "I don't think I'd better have any more alcohol."

"Yeah, I noticed you staggering around on the dance floor."

"I overheat is the problem. My body temperature goes up. I feel like I have the flu or something."

"All right. Next round I'll order milk."

She smiled and said, "Are we going back to your place?"

"If you want to."

"A part of me wants to."

"Which part is that?"

"You know what I mean."

"You mean," I said, "you're not sure if you want to go back to my place or not. Whether things are moving too fast. Whether you're ready. Whether *I'm* ready. And that's very natural."

"Oh, it is, doctor? And how did you come by all this medical knowledge?"

"I went to the library and read up on breast cancer."

"Are you serious?"

"Spent an hour there."

"God, Sam."

"And part of what I read was that you'd just naturally be uneasy about—"

"You really went to the library?"

I was trying to tell if she was amused or angry. I couldn't.

She said, "Were there pictures?"

"Photographs, you mean?"

"Yes."

"Uh-huh. There were."

"Of—after surgery?"

"Of after surgery."

"I don't know if I like that, Sam."

"I'll tell you what. Let's dance again."

"Now?"

"Nat 'King' Cole. C'mon."

We danced. In fact, we danced to the next three records, all ballads. And said not a word. She didn't hold me quite so tightly now. And when I accidentally stepped on her foot, she didn't make any kind of smart remark.

She said, "I wish you hadn't done that."

"Gone to the library?"

"Yes."

"But I was just—"

"I know what you were trying to do, Sam. And it's sweet, it really is. To care about me that much. But I don't want you to see me as some kind of freak you need to read up on."

Then she put her head on my shoulder and held me very tight indeed and when I started to say something, she said, "Please don't say anything, Sam. Please don't."

"I'm drunk already," she said as she stood up. And she was, in fact, a tad wobbly as she headed for the second time to the john. "I must have a bladder the size of a pea."

We'd come back to my apartment and despite her earlier resolution to forsake the bottle, she'd been matching me drink for drink. That sounds more impressive than it is, given the fact that I'm a terrible drinker. We'd had two more drinks was all. She went into the john and while I waited for her, I put my head back and tried to remember what it was like the first time I ever got drunk. Either it was when I snuck a quart of Hamms from the refrigerator and slept out in a tent with Mike Totter when we were fourteen; or it was the time Dodie McKay invited me over— I was fifteen—when her folks were out of town. The thing with the quart of beer was that I was also smoking cigarettes and the combination made me really giddy for a long time and then made me vomit. I'm not sure I was drunk, I think I just tested the limits of my stomach. With Dodie, I got drunk enough that I told her how much I loved the beautiful Pamela Forrest and would always love the beautiful Pamela Forrest and if there was an afterlife I would love the beautiful Pamela Forrest then, too. None of which Dodie wanted to hear. She'd invited me over to see if I wanted to go to the freshman dance, an invitation she took back by the end of the evening when she put me on the street to wobble my way home.

It was like a first drunk tonight, that was the best way to describe it. New and novel and giggly as hell.

When Linda came out of the bathroom, she headed straight for my chair. "Okay if I turn all the lights out?"

"What if I'm afraid of the dark?"

"Tough."

So she went around and turned the lights out and then came over and sat in my lap. It was great there in the dark with her, the feel and smell and womanness and girliness of her, the feel of her hose and the perfect length of neck and the toothpaste scent fresh from my bathroom, a little squeeze of my Colgate no doubt.

"I used to sit in my Dad's lap when I was little and comb his hair all forward. And then I'd laugh and laugh."

"Do you want to comb my hair all forward?"

She reached up and clipped off the lamp on the end table next to the armchair we sat in. And that was when she kissed me.

The moonlight cast everything into silver and shadow relief. The apartment had never looked better.

I let her slide back on me and then I slipped my arm around her back. I didn't realize she had shorn herself of bra until my hand reached the middle of her spine.

She did it quickly, deftly, while she was still kissing me, unbuttoned her blouse. My hand found its way to her breast and touched it with a kind of lusty fondness or fond lustiness. Take your choice.

She sighed deeply, tilted her head back. "That feels so good."

"I'm used to seeing you fishing off that deserted railroad bridge in the summer," I said. "You always wore white T-shirts without a bra. I always wanted you to stand at an angle to the sun so I could get a glimpse of your breasts."

"Why didn't you ever ask me out, Sam?" She took my hand and kissed it and then placed it on her breast again.

"I was too busy with the Queen of Sheba."

"The beautiful Pamela Forrest."

"Unfortunately, yes."

"You really think you're over her?"

"I'm pretty sure."

"That's good enough for me."

She tilted my face up and kissed me again. "I'm really getting into the mood now. I wasn't sure I could."

"Yeah, so am I."

This time, I kissed her. Teenage lust did wonderful and urgent things to my crotch. There's nothing like good old teenage lust when you're in your twenties. Long may it last.

I knew the rules for tonight. The skirt wouldn't come off let alone the slip and the panties. Nice and slow and easy. With an emphasis on slow.

But we sure found a lot of things to do within the limits of the rules, let me tell you. You reach a point in foreplay when you think you just may need to be committed to a mental hospital, you're that goofy.

And then the moment was there. I don't know why it was the moment—there hadn't been anything said, she hadn't urged my hand in any particular direction—but it was the moment and it was time to do it.

I wanted to do it when we were in the depths of a kiss that was making us thrusting gasping maniacs, because then it would be natural.

And it was natural. I just slipped my hand over. The nerve endings on my palm registered data with my brain—the shock of feeling the thin coarse patterns of the scarring where her

breast had been. I wanted to tell myself—tell her—that everything was just fine, that it was just a little scarring was all. No
big deal.

But of course it was a big deal. It would take some getting used
to. As would looking at it in the light sometime.

But then I thought of what this moment must be like for her.
How much she'd dreaded it, yet had wanted to get it over with.
And how, based on my reading at the library, her future was
perilous. The recovery rate for her kind of breast cancer was
not good.

She started crying, not hard, not dramatic, and put her head on
my shoulder, her tears warm on the side of my neck.

After a time, she raised her head and said, "You want another
drink?"

"Not right now."

"Me neither, I guess."

She eased herself onto my lap again and I slipped my arms
around her.

After a time she said: "I meet with this group of women
who've had the same kind of surgery. There're some men who
can't handle it."

"Then they're not men worth knowing. You're still yourself.
That's what matters."

"Please don't lie to me, Sam."

"I'm not lying. I'm not saying it was easy here tonight. I really
was afraid I'd do or say something wrong. But a lot of times the
fear is worse than the reality. I'm just happy I finally got to see
one of those breasts you used to flaunt at me down at the railroad bridge."

"Oh, yes, I'm the flaunting type, all right. Roger Darcy was the
only boy I would've flaunted myself around."

"Roger Darcy? The kid who used to call in all those false fire alarms?"

"I felt sorry for him."

"Roger Darcy. He's probably an arsonist by now." A merry kiss of her doing, and once again we went at it, determined to find out just how much you could get away with within tonight's rules.

You'd be surprised how much fun you can have within those rules.

TWENTY

As you're breathing your last, say a quick prayer that the priest who buries you is Father Mulcahy and not Father Fitzpatrick.

David Egan had always claimed to be unlucky. And his unluck held right to the end. Father Fitzpatrick presided over his funeral mass and burial.

Father Peter Fitzpatrick was once a real sharp priest. This was probably sometime around the Civil War. He'd served in several larger cities and then gotten himself sent here instead of retiring. He always said he didn't want to retire. He was a priest on the model of MGM central casting priests—white-haired, pleasantly overweight, with a radiant smile for everybody.

The problem was he'd never bothered to get to know anybody here. He mostly played golf in the warm months and went to movies in the cooler ones. He'd found a way of retiring without retiring. Since there were only two priests, he had to take his share of funerals and his words on the deceased were always masterpieces of ham-bone rhetoric.

In Father Fitzgerald's Generic Speech for the Recently Departed, everybody had led an exemplary life, had been universally beloved and was certainly, even as we sat squirming in our pews, sitting next to God and enjoying a Western on the celestial TV set, Father Fitzpatrick being partial to Westerns.

Of David Egan, he said: "People always knew they could come to David Egan if they had problems of a spiritual nature. And with them he shared his knowledge of right and wrong, and how to survive these troubled times with hope and humility."

Sounded just like the David I knew.

I couldn't listen to the rest. I'd heard this same sermon applied to a wife-beating drunk, a twenty-year-old girl of saintly soul and beauty who had died of a brain aneurysm, a crooked and vicious cop, a kind and gentle man who ran a flower shop and was the subject of much rumor because he was unmarried at age fifty, and a decent old bullshitter from County Cork who'd lost both legs on Guam in the worst days of World War II.

Hell, Father Fitzpatrick would've repeated those same words— "he shared his knowledge of right and wrong" and taught "them how to survive these troubled times with hope and humility"—if he'd been burying Heinrich Himmler.

The back rows of the church were packed with young people who were angling for a role in *Danger Dolls!* about hot-rodding girl gangs. David's friends. The ones he'd taught about right and wrong.

The front rows were crowded with the more reputable friends he'd made in his high school days. The girls cried, the boys looked bored, though there was one boy who managed to cry *and* look bored at the same time, no easy feat, believe me.

But the people I spent the most time watching were the Kelly sisters, sitting in the front pew on the right side of the aisle, and the two girls sitting a mere row apart on the left side of the aisle, Molly Blessing and Rita Scully. They both wore dark suits and looked quite pretty and young and forlorn. The Kelly sisters used Kleenex to daub their eyes; the girls used delicate handkerchiefs.

Father Fitzpatrick droned through his sermon, dragged through the rest of the mass, and then walked down to the communion rail to commence escorting the coffin out to the waiting hearse. The rows emptied from front to back. I was near the middle so I didn't get out in time to actually see it. But I heard about it, of course.

Sunny day. Cars whipping by, the drivers indifferent—or frightened by—this death in their midst. Small clutches of mourners on the sidewalk, talking, a smile dared here and there, and then the shout.

I had just reached the center of the front steps when Rita slapped Molly or Molly slapped Rita and the fight ensued. I've heard the story told both ways. Personally, I'd put my money on Rita as the instigator, but then you can't automatically dismiss the quiet ones like Molly, because sometimes they have tempers worthy of Charles Starkweather.

I did get to see the last few seconds of it, the part when Rita reached over and grabbed the shoulder of Molly's suit and started ripping away. Which when about 673 guys jumped in between them and the bell sounded, officially ending the fight.

Talk about your town legends. This would be talked about for generations. And it was just the sort of thing Egan would have loved, two very attractive girls battling over him this way.

They were both red-faced, sweaty, and thoroughly disheveled by the time I got over there. I didn't get to talk to either of them. They were both dragged away by their friends.

I'm happy to report that there were no fisticuffs at the burial site, though Father Fitzpatrick did get confused once and talked about "David's courage in fighting in Korea." David would've been about eight back then. Well, at least he hadn't put him back in World War I.

I'd hoped to see Andrea Prescott. At the moment the person I was most curious about was Jack Coyle. I'd wasted our little confrontation because I hadn't pushed any specifics at him. I wanted to know where he and Sara met when they got together.

Andrea Prescott was in Iowa City, in class all day, her mother told me. The mom was much nicer than the daughter. I told her I'd try her later.

I spent two hours in the office trying to make some real money. I was finishing up with a probated will when I thought I might learn something from Kenny Chesmore.

"How's it going, Kenny?"

"Two more chapters, man. Lesbians are a lot easier to write about than three-ways."

"Those damned three-ways. They can wear a guy out."

"I'm in kind of a hurry here, McCain. What's up?"

"If you wanted to take an eighteen-year-old girl to a motel within driving distance of town here, where would you take her?"

"Eighteen? She's legal, anyway."

"Barely," I said.

"That's a pun but I'll let it pass."

Kenny knew how much I hated puns.

"What you're really saying is where could you take her where nobody at the motel would talk, right?"

"Right."

"Nowhere."

"What's that mean?"

"It means they all blab. All the owners, all the night clerks. When I get stuck for ideas sometimes, I call them up and they tell me about some of the kinky stuff their customers do."

"So you can't think of any place?"

"I'd go private. If it were a steady thing, I'd have a little apartment stuck away somewhere. Something like that. Or I'd take her along with me on business trips. But no way would I start jumping her anywhere around here. Somebody'd spot you for sure."

"Well, thanks, Kenny."

"Sure. This thing you're working on, McCain. It wouldn't involve a three-way, would it?"

"May all your future books involve lesbians, my son."

"Thank you, padre."

I tried working again but couldn't concentrate, especially after Jamie came in with one of her girlfriends, whom she insisted was going to help her make some serious headway on all the filing she'd neglected for the past month. The friend was a ponytailed girl with earnest eyeglasses and a sweet serious face. Under her left arm were two books, *Tender Is the Night* by F. Scott Fitzgerald and *Down and Out in Paris and London* by George Orwell. And she was hanging out with Jamie?

"This is my cousin Carrie, Mr. C. She gets straight As."

I reached out and we shook hands. She glanced at Jamie and said, "I just realized something, Jamie."

Jamie was pushing a ball of pink bubblegum into her erotic mouth. "Realized what, Carrie?"

"If Mr. McCain's name starts with 'M' why do you call him 'Mr. C.'?"

Jamie looked half offended that anybody could possibly be daft enough to ask such a question. "Because they call Perry Como Mr. C." *My God, Carrie, what are you, an idiot?*

Carrie rolled her eyes and said, "Boy, I can see what you meant about the filing. It's kind of a mess." She walked over to the window and dragged a long finger through a quarter inch of dust. "Could stand a little cleaning, too."

"I promised Mr. C I'd sort of clean things up after my hands heal." Jamie dangled her hands in front of us. "I was using this Rexall lotion my mom bought me. I wanted to throw it away—I mean, Rexall makes beauty products?—but I used it because she's always talking about how I waste money and I get real sick of hearing that speech. But look at my hands now."

I looked at her hands. Her cousin Carrie looked at her hands. I looked at Carrie and Carrie looked at me and then we both looked back at Jamie and Carrie said, "Your hands look fine."

"To you, maybe, they look fine. But I have to wear them everyday. And believe me, they look terrible after using that Rexall junk. So I have to wait till they're healed again before I can do any, you know, like *cleaning* or anything. Typing, no problem. Answering the phone, no problem. Getting Mr. C some coffee from down the street, no problem. But cleaning—not for a while."

Two-hour lunches with Turk, no problem. Tying up the office phone gossiping with her girlfriends, no problem. Misspelling every other word in business letters, no problem. But cleaning—

"Well," I said, "I appreciate you coming in, Carrie. Is forty cents an hour all right?"

"Oh, I don't want any pay, Mr. McCain. I get class credit for doing this. I'm taking business courses."

"I'm going to teach her how to type," Jamie said.

Carrie winked at me. "Yes, I've seen Jamie type. It's really something."

I liked this girl already.

"Well," Carrie said. "Time to get to work."

"Yes," Jamie sighed. "That's about all we do around here, isn't it, Mr. C? Work, work, work."

The poor dear girl.

* * *

She sat with her tan suede desert boots up on the edge of the desk, some kind of black stuff staining a quarter inch of them above the sole. Donny Hughes would be glad to know she was wearing them. I assumed these were the ones he'd gifted her with.

She had an ancient stand-up phone in one hand while the other hand held the receiver to her ear. She said, "Mrs. Russell, Calamity's getting old. None of us wants to face that but we have to. I know your boys don't think he's 'exciting' anymore, but if you want 'something to happen to him,' you'll have to do it yourself. I couldn't do that. I see Calamity every day. I love him. So you think about it and if you want your boys to get a new horse, fine, I'll help you get one, but I sure won't help Calamity have an 'accident.' Good-bye, Mrs. Russell." Rita Scully replaced receiver on hook, phone on desk, set her feet on the floor and said, "She wants me to kill her horse. It's been in the family for ten years, ever since her twins were four years old. Now the boys want something younger and faster but she doesn't want to pay for two stalls, so she wants me to stage an accident so Calamity won't be a financial drain anymore. Nice folks out there. Say, McCain, you got a smoke? I'm plumb out."

"Well, lucky for you, I'm not plumb out."

I pitched her my pack and my lighter. She grinned. "I pick up words from cowboys at the rodeo. Hence, plumb."

"So which word did you pick up from the rodeo, 'hence' or 'plumb'?"

She slid the pack and lighter back across the desk. She took a big gulp of cancer and exhaled it right at where I sat on the customer side of the desk. "Did little Molly send you out here to make me apologize?"

"Haven't seen Molly since the funeral."

She wore a black Western shirt with white piping and some lovingly fitted jeans. "I used to beat the crap out of my older brother. My mom said that when boys found that out they'd never take me to dances."

"They'd be afraid you'd beat them up, too?"

"No, they wouldn't want to be seen in public with anybody so unladylike is what my mom had in mind. But then I got finished with my braces and lost the fat in my cheeks and this body came along out of nowhere. Boys begged me to go to dances."

"And they say this isn't a great country."

The humor in her eyes vanished so completely it was hard to believe it was ever there. "Molly killed David, you know."

"And how would that be?"

"The pressure she put him under. Constant pressure to marry her."

"She thought she could help him."

She shrugged. "Everybody thought they could help him." She looked around the office. Framed black-and-white photos of various horses covered the walls as did numerous, and dusty, framed awards. There was another cluttered, battered desk like hers in the corner with another old-fashioned phone and two filing cabinets that looked even older than mine. Hay from the stables covered the floor. The two windows were almost dirty enough to pass as walls. The rest was the usual tack room stuff competing for space with the office—brass hooks with bridles and reins and bits hanging from them; and saddle racks made from reinforced sawhorses that would support the heavy saddles. Along the floor on the east wall were several pairs of Western boots. What I was most curious about were the chaps. I wondered if she ever wore them.

She said, "We make a nice living here. I hope to raise my kids here. When David was sober and thinking straight, he wanted to live here, too." She took a bitter drag of her smoke. "But Molly and Sara—they made him feel like somebody important. That's the one thing I couldn't give him. I know who I am and what I am. I'm nobody important according to our little burg here. And I also know that you can't force a guy into marrying you."

She stubbed out her cigarette. "Got another one?"

I pushed the pack to her. "How'd you end up with David on Saturday night?"

"I saw him cruising around. He looked pretty bombed. I told him he'd better let me drive or Cliffie'd get him for sure."

"What time did you see him?"

"Eight or so. Why?"

"I'm just trying to reconstruct his day and his night."

"Can his aunts help you?"

"That's where I'm headed after this." Then, "You think Donny Hughes could've killed him?" I hadn't told her about Brenda Carlyle.

She lighted her second cigarette. "He hated David, that's for sure. There's just one thing wrong." She smiled coldly. "You really think he'd have the nerve to do something like that? Little Donny Hughes?"

It was one of those moments when you realize that somewhere, sometime, a woman smiled like that about you. And that you, in turn, sometime, somewhere, smiled that way about a woman.

"He's in love with you."

"Yes, and he never lets me forget it, either. I shouldn't have talked about him that way. He's nice but it'll be a long time before—" She shrugged. "He'll make somebody a nice husband."

"I take it that's not a quality you're especially interested in at the moment."

"I told you, I want kids and a family life. But that doesn't mean I'm willing to settle for some timid little guy who lets me walk all over him."

I stood up and walked back to the door. She watched me, her dark gaze impossible to read. She was a formidable young woman.

I said, "You happen to remember where you were Friday night?"

"Are you asking me if I killed Sara, McCain?"

"Something like that, I guess."

"Well, I'll tell you something. I thought about it enough. I thought about each and every one of the girls he threw me over for. He almost always came back, though. Even with Molly, he came back. Even with Princess Sara, he came back." This time the cold smile was for herself. "The trouble was that the bastard never stayed long." Then, "Just a sec, I'll walk out with you. I need to change boots. These ones Donny gave me are a half size too small. Isn't that just like him?"

Sweet Emma and sweet Amy were sitting out on their porch glider. Emma was reading the paper and Amy was darning socks. One of their cats sat on the porch railing watching me. The day was starting the long stretch into dusk, the shadows deep and somehow lonely, a certain melancholy creeping into the laughter of kids playing in a nearby front yard. All too soon moms in aprons would be on front porches calling them in for supper, wash-those-hands-first, as the first stars came out and the night grew chill. A clunker Plymouth packed with teenagers raced by, Elvis way up high.

You could see Amy had been crying. David would never leave this house. Not except in body.

"Good afternoon, ladies."

"Good afternoon, Sam." They both spoke as one and then smiled at each other about it.

Emma said, "We got his room all ready for you yesterday, but with all the excitement about Brenda. . . ."

"Well, you had time to hide all the evidence, that's for sure."

Amy said, "We didn't throw anything away. We really didn't, Sam."

"But you do have a secret, right?"

"How did you know?" Amy said.

Emma scolded her sister with a hard blue glance. "Now he knows we *have* a secret, Amy. Thanks to you."

"He already knew we had a secret, didn't you, Sam?"

"Well, the way you made such a fuss about cleaning it up, I figured something was going on."

"It's nothing we're proud of, believe me, Sam," Emma said.

"Well, I didn't notice you turning any of it down last night, if you're so ashamed of it, sister."

Nice to know that even saintly women got into the occasional blood feud.

"Do I get to know what you're talking about?"

"Would you like some lemonade, Sam? I made it from fresh lemons about an hour ago."

"No thanks, Emma. But I would like to know what you two are talking about."

The sisters looked at each other and then back at me.

"Why don't you go up to his room and look through things," Emma said, "and give us a little more time to talk through this stuff."

"So I don't get to know what all this is about?" I kept my tone light but I really was curious.

"You go up and look through his room," Amy said, "and we'll decide if we're going to tell you or not. It's—nothing we're proud of, Sam."

I smiled. Sitting on their glider. Darning socks. Sweet as a sentimental magazine illustration. What kind of secret could they have?

"You wouldn't be communist spies, would you?"

Emma: "Oh, Sam."

"Or be running a bawdy house?"

Amy: "Sam, what a dirty mind you have."

"Or be running a white slavery ring?"

"Help yourself to the lemonade if you want, Sam. You know where the refrigerator is."

I passed on the lemonade, making my way up the interior stairs to the second floor and David's room. Instead of teenage idol pics, his walls were covered with hot rods. Street rods, most of them, mostly Fords from the 1930s cut down and sculpted into mythic beasts of style and grace. His small bookcase held hot-rod magazines arranged carefully by date, and a dozen or so paperbacks lurid of cover and violent of copy: "Speed, switchblades . . . and sex! Today's teens on the prowl!" They seemed to be the prose equivalent of drive-in movies. Egan had no doubt identified with the troubled protagonists.

Closet, desk, bureau didn't reveal anything useful. His aunts bought most of his clothes at Sears; his better shirts—presumably he'd chosen them himself—had come from J. C. Penney's.

Underneath the desk were two shoeboxes I hadn't noticed while I'd been looking through the drawers. I drew them out and sat down on the bed and went through their contents. I looked out at the dusky sky. I wondered how many times Egan had sat on this bed staring out at the same backyard-garage-alley scene. It was a comforting sight. Home in a small town. I wondered if he'd taken solace in it or if his bitterness and self-pity had made peace impossible for him.

The first box contained maybe four dozen photographs of hot cars he'd taken at the drag strip in Cordoba, Illinois. It was in the second box that I found the love letters.

I spent half an hour going through them, interrupted twice by yoo-hoos shouted up the stairs by the Kelly sisters. Was everything all right? Did I want to stay to supper? Was I sure I didn't want some fresh-squeezed lemonade?

The letters came from a dozen different girls in Black River Falls and a few surrounding towns. He'd taken his show on the road, apparently. Most of them were awkward and pained of expression, and heartbreaking in their earnest pleas for his attention and love. I could imagine him sitting in his room late at night, beyond the comfort of liquor and easy sex, making himself feel better by going through these letters. It wasn't as simple as egotism. Not with the life he'd had. These were objective affirmations of his worth and for the first time I felt as sorry for him as I did for the girls who'd loved him. To at least a few people in this life, he mattered. He was the somebody he'd always longed to be.

The most literate letters were from Molly. She reminded him that she had loved him since that time in seventh grade when he'd asked her to slow dance at a school mixer. She reminded him of how she'd been able to get him to cut way back on his drinking and how she'd convinced him to go to the board of education soon and see how he should go about taking a high school equivalency test. Rita's were rock-and-roll treatises that sounded very much like the copy on the paperback covers . . . speed, switchblades, and sex. She shared his "greed for speed" and enjoyed all the "wild and dangerous places" they'd made love in. And like Molly, she reminded him that she'd loved him a long time, too, since ninth grade and that he was only truly himself when he was with her. Rita mentioned that she'd even given up her best friend Molly because of him.

At the bottom of the box were a few dozen photographs of Egan in his school days. The pictures told the tale. Half of them featured Molly, the other half Rita. Despite this obvious rivalry, neither had ever thrown him over. I thought about my waning addiction to the beautiful—and absent—Pamela Forrest. Sometimes you're the only one who doesn't know she's never going to fall in love with you.

The two girls were more interesting to look at than Egan. He'd always looked pretty much the same. He'd aspired to James Deanhood since 1955, when Dean became a popular actor.

But the girls . . . for such beauties, neither had been especially pretty in young girlhood. Their bloom would come later. Molly had enough braces on her teeth to shred a car fender and was thin to the point of looking like a poster kid encouraging you to stamp out world hunger; Rita was plump and squinty-eyed and unsmiling. There was a kind of symbiosis here, the three of them. There was even one photo—they were in maybe seventh grade— of the three of them together, one girl on each side of him, a tetherball pole in the background, the girls smiling as if they were friends. They all had one thing in common: David Egan was the center of their lives.

I found the half-smoked marijuana stick on the bottom of the box. The grass was fresh as I squeezed it. Egan must have stashed his contraband in here. I'd tried the stuff a number of times in Iowa City but I always had the same reaction I did to booze. It put me to sleep.

When I went downstairs, the ladies were on the living room couch watching a quiz show with Garry Moore. I carried the box over and showed them the half joint in the box. "You know what this is, ladies?"

Amy said, "Oh, Lord, sister, I told you he'd find out."

"So you knew he was smoking marijuana?"

"We're not addicts, Sam," Amy said. "We just tried it a few times."

"Amy," Emma said, "will you please be still? Sam just wanted to know if we knew that David smoked it."

"Wait a minute," I said, "you mean you were smoking it, too?" I couldn't help smiling. I tried to imagine these two elderly Irish ladies, mass-goers seven days a week, smoking a reefer.

"We just tried a few of his sticks was all," Emma said.

"He talked us into it, Sam."

Emma said, "He was always talking us into things. He'd get us a little tipsy once in a while. Or he'd teach us some new dance step while he played some of his records. Or he'd get us to watch some naughty movie on TV."

"He said we had to know what was going on in the world. He got a big kick out of it. He wasn't in a good mood all that often—especially near the end of his life—so we went along with it."

"Seeing him happy made *us* happy, Sam," Emma said.

I looked at one face and then the other. I could see them now in the newspaper: SAINTLY OLD LADIES ARRESTED FOR SMOKING REEFERS.

I laughed. "Well, did you enjoy it?"

They glanced at each other.

"Sort of," Emma said.

"Not that we'd ever do it again," Amy said.

"It mostly made us hungry the three times we smoked it," Emma said. "We made this huge chocolate cake."

"It was the first lopsided cake Emma ever made. Marijuana kind of confuses you."

"So," Emma said, obviously wanting to change the subject. "Did you find anything else?"

"Letters and photos."

"He sure kept a lot of them, didn't he?" Emma said.

"Did either Molly or Rita come over here much?"

"Oh, sure," Emma said. "All the time. They were all good friends at one time."

"That's why Molly hated her so much, I think," Amy said.

"She felt betrayed, I guess. She used to bring Rita along when they were in ninth grade. Then David and Rita started sneaking off together. I felt so sorry for Molly."

"I did, too," Emma said, "up until she smashed all the windows out in their cars."

"Molly smashed out windows?"

"Isn't that something?" Amy said. "You'd never think anybody like her could do something like that. But she was heartbroken." She spent a moment gazing at the past. "A long, long time ago, and I'm sure Emma will remember this, I went out with this Nabisco salesman from Davenport. He'd come to town once a week. I had a head full of silly notions. The silliest being that he would marry me someday. I eventually found out he was married."

"You wonder why we ended up old maids, Sam? That's why. I had a similar experience. Mine wasn't married. But he wasn't true blue, either. Hers was 1939 and mine was 1941. We decided then to stay with our parents and work at our little jobs—we both worked in dime stores back then—and never be hurt again."

"So I could see why Molly did what she did, Sam," Amy said.

"So could I," Emma said and smiled at her sister. "And I'm supposed to be the 'sensible' one. Molly probably didn't think she was being very sensible but I'm sure she was having a good time smashing in those windows."

Amy grinned. "Why, look at his face, sister. He's shocked. First, he finds out that his favorite two old maids smoke marijuana. And now he has to listen to us condoning smashing in car windows."

"I'll never recover," I said. And I half wondered if I would. People become fixed points in your life, like stars. But sometimes you find out that they aren't as fixed as you thought. "You don't chop up people and keep them in the basement, do you?"

"We'll invite you over for a delicious 'meat' dish some night," Emma said deadpan.

"Emma!"

"I'd keep an eye on that sister of yours, Amy," I said as I was leaving.

"Don't worry, Sam, I do."

"Don't forget that special meat dinner of ours," Emma said. Amy slapped playfully at her arm.

TWENTY-ONE

ANDREA PRESCOTT'S MOTHER DIDN'T sound so happy to hear from me this time. Apparently her daughter had been helping her bone up on how to be snotty on the phone. "I'm not sure I want her to talk to you."

"It's really important."

"To you, maybe, Mr. McCain. But we're respectable people and we don't want to get dragged into anything having to do with that terrible David Egan."

"I may not be respectable, Mrs. Prescott, but I am trying to find the proof."

"That was an awfully stuffy thing to say, don't you think?"

I laughed. I sort of liked her again. "Yeah, come to think of it it was. I must've heard that in a movie or something."

She sounded much friendlier. "A very bad movie, Mr. McCain." Then, "You may speak to her for two minutes and no longer."

"You going to run an egg timer?"

"I have a watch and believe it or not, I know how to tell time." Then, "Here, honey."

"I wish you'd quit bugging me," the girl said to me.

"Nice to speak with you again, too, Andrea."

"I told you what I know and Mom and Dad wish I hadn't even told you that much."

"Jack Coyle was seeing her again, wasn't he? He broke it off for a long time but then he started seeing her again, didn't he?"

"I'm going to hang up now."

"And the baby wasn't David's, it was Coyle's, wasn't it."

"Good-bye, McCain."

"Where did they meet? They couldn't go to a motel. That'd be too dangerous. But they had some rendezvous spot, didn't they?"

She hesitated. Then whispered. "Mom just went into the kitchen. She really doesn't want me to get involved. But I'll tell you this. There's a hunting cabin out by Scarecrow Rock. Sara mentioned it once to me." Hesitation. "That's what they were fighting about the night before she got killed. She was still in love with Coyle and it was driving David crazy."

I heard footsteps and then her mother say, "Tell Mr. McCain that my egg timer just went off."

"Thanks for the help, Andrea. I appreciate it."

I guess if you lie flat on your back and look straight up at it and the moonlight behind it is just right and the night is cloudless and if you really use your imagination, you can kinda sorta perhaps see how this tall, slender piece of red limestone came to be called Scarecrow Rock. One night in high school when I was particularly brokenhearted over the beautiful Pamela Forrest, I lay on the ground and did exactly that. And in my drunken state of poetic heartbreak, lying right at the base of the damned thing, I could indeed kinda sorta see how it did, if you closed one eye, more or less look vaguely like a scarecrow. I have spent my time in this vale of tears wisely, wasting not a moment.

It didn't look at all like a scarecrow tonight. A small forest. A moonlit mesa. A five-foot-tall piece of limestone jutting up from a limestone base almost blood-red in this light. A buck deer heard me, pausing momentarily on the mesa and then fleeing with the fragile grace of its kind.

The mesa came at the end of what locals called the Comanche Trail. If you read much about the Comanches, it's hard to believe they ever got as far east as Iowa. But somehow the narrow, winding dirt trail got itself named that and the locals liked it enough to keep it, accurate history be damned. In true pioneer spirit, I stopped to take a pee a couple of times, stoke up a Lucky, and get whipped hard enough by sharp-edged pine branches to draw a little blood on my forehead. I also kept stumbling. I wondered if the pioneers had worn penny loafers. Probably, wouldn't you think?

River smell. A lone motorboat somewhere in the darkness. The trail would soon swing northwest, away from the river where, as I recalled, I'd find the hunting cabin.

I had to make a trail of my own, straight down through the loamed and leafy undergrowth you find in any deep woods, the mixed scent of mint and mud and a million feces samples from the little ones—foxes and rabbits and possums and raccoons, among them—whose gleaming eyes followed me as I tripped and stumbled downslope toward another trail that would take me to the cabin. I hoped I was giving them enough entertainment to last them for a while. That I know of, they don't have TV.

I ended my downslope travels with an homage to Buster Keaton. My foot got lodged in a massive claw root extending from a tree. Yanking it free, I stumbled the edge of the slope and fell headfirst to the trail three feet below.

I banged my head hard enough against the earth of the trail to knock myself out momentarily. I also embarrassed the hell out of myself. I could hear the owls laughing now.

I got up, lit a Lucky, and started walking again. Low-hanging pine branches slapping me from either side. The trail angled upward abruptly. At the top of the rise I stood looking down on the cabin I was looking for.

I've never figured out why they call these things cabins. It's really a summer house. Two stories, screened-in front porch, one-car garage. The pioneers, the people who really did live in cabins and soddies, would have called this a mansion.

When I got up close, standing on the beach in front of the place, I found that the garage was empty and the front door locked. No lights inside. All I could hear was the river rushing past thirty yards away. A half-moon had risen above a tiny, nearby island, tall ragged pines silhouetted against its glow.

I stayed on the front porch for a time, squinting inside through the large windows on either side of the door. A nicely furnished place, from what I could see. Large, native stone fireplace, leather furnishings, and a spectacular display of animal heads on the wall, everything from moose to bobcat, spectacular if you weren't one of those displayed, anyway.

It was time for drastic measures. I took out my Swiss Army knife, which at last count had something like 2,347,000 uses and cost only $2.99 if you also included the coupon the pulp magazine provided.

I started walking around the house, carrying an empty wooden Pepsi case to stand on, looking for a window I could pry open. Two baby raccoons watched me from a tree limb, their bottoms hanging below the limb, their tails twitching kittenlike.

As it turned out, I didn't need to use my Swiss Army knife. One of the back windows had been left unlocked. I set the Pepsi case up. It was wobbly but it stayed upright long enough for me to grab the window ledge and pull myself inside.

Tobacco. Whiskey. Coldness. These were the things I smelled

immediately. The deeper I went into the shadowy house, the more the odors shifted. A recent meal, fried meat, probably beef. Then—coffee percolating in the dark kitchen. Somebody here. Shampoo in the downstairs bathroom. A scent of perfume on the stairway leading to the second floor.

I stood on the landing, not sure where to start. The downstairs hadn't given me anything. I was self-conscious. My breathing sounded too loud. And wherever I stepped, the flooring squeaked. Then the dust of the place made me sneeze. A cat burglar I was not.

There were four doors, two on each side of the hall. The first door opened on a dormitory-like bedroom. Two pairs of bunkbeds, a bureau with a clock radio on top, a closet where various hunters over the years had left odds and ends of their pleasure, a couple of duck calls, a camouflage jacket, a rain hat, a pair of waders that I associated more with fishing than hunting. In other words, nothing.

Same setup in the next room, the pair of bunkbeds, the bureau, the dormlike configurations. Maybe these middle-aged men missed college life and these cramped little rooms brought back all kinds of remembered pleasures.

I was just leaving this room when Jean Coyle appeared in the moonlit doorway and said, "You shouldn't be here, Sam. You're trespassing."

The moonlight gave her an ethereal presence. But the black steel gun in her hand kept her very real. Even though I've carried a gun sometimes, being around them still spooks me. At least she wasn't pointing it at me.

"You shouldn't be here, Sam." Her voice was dulled. Exhaustion, maybe; alcohol.

"Are you all right?"

"Do I look all right, Sam?"

"I wish you didn't have that gun, Jean."

"I heard somebody breaking in. I knew where Jack keeps it in the bedroom down the hall."

"I'm just doing my job."

The way she half slumped against the doorframe, I decided it was exhaustion not liquor that had sapped her energy. In her sporty suburban jacket, blouse, and slacks, she still looked vivacious in her languid way. But it was the vivacity of a mannequin.

"You're trying to blame Jack, aren't you?"

"I don't know who I'm trying to blame, Jean."

"How much do you know?"

"He used to bring Sara Griffin here. I know that much." I hesitated to tell her that the child Sara had been carrying was perhaps Jack's. I wasn't sure she could handle it right now.

She pitched forward. I reached her in time to keep her upright. I lifted her up in my arms and carried her down the stairs. She probably weighed around one hundred fifteen. I had to keep redoubling my arm strength. I was pretty wobbly getting her down the steps.

The leather couch near the fireplace was big enough to work as a daybed. There was even a red woolen football-game blanket at one end of it. I got her arranged and went for some of the coffee I'd smelled earlier.

I found the liquor while I was in the kitchen. I grabbed a fifth of Wild Turkey on my way back to the living room. After I got her sitting up high enough to drink the Irish coffee without choking, I got the lights on and found the thermostat. Deep in the metal bowels of a furnace came the promise of heat.

I lighted a cigarette and poured myself a thumb of whiskey. I sat in a chair across from the couch. I felt like her inquisitor. I didn't have any choice.

"Was he in love with her?"

"Thanks for taking care of me."

"We're friends, Jean. What the hell else would I do?"

She sipped. "This tastes very good." She huddled her hands around the cup as if she were very cold. "That was the first part of the explanation. That he was in love with her. But that was the first time."

"The first time?"

"When she was younger. Worked part-time in his office. And they had an affair. He knew it would destroy both of them so he broke it off. That's when she had her breakdown and went into the mental hospital. She would never tell her parents who she'd had the affair with. And they never figured it out. They might have suspected but they didn't have any proof."

"And you took him back?"

She smiled sadly. "I'm a forgiving person, Sam. It's my nature. I can't help it. He made a mistake and asked me if I could forgive him. I did."

"Wasn't it difficult?"

"Difficult?" The sad smile again. "Two or three times a day I'd have these little breakdowns. I'd be furious or I'd be so depressed I was paralyzed. I don't think I let him touch me for a year. And I mean not even a friendly kiss. I just kept thinking how old I must look to him after Sara. She was so beautiful. I even tried a psychologist in Cedar Rapids. The most vain man I've ever met. He thought it would be good for me if I went to bed with him. He sat down next to me once and tried to kiss me. I walked out and never went back. He had nerve enough to send me a bill. Which I didn't pay, of course."

She drank more coffee. Held the empty cup up. "Do you suppose I could get a refill?"

"Get your own damned coffee."

For just an instant she believed me and looked shocked. Then she laughed. Or tried to. "I forgot about your sense of humor, Sam. How deadpan you can be."

After I brought her a second cup, and after I was sitting down again, she said, "About four or five months ago—I can't say for sure exactly when—Sara started calling Jack again. I actually felt sorry for her. She was obsessed with him. All that time in the mental hospital—she hadn't improved any at all. She'd just managed to stay away from him, but once she gave in to the urge again, she started following him. Calling him. Sending him love letters. And then waiting for him in his car at his office. He couldn't get away from her. And then—" Her hands huddled around her coffee cup again. Her gaze was fixed on the past. She said. "He gave in to her one night. She convinced him to come out here to the cabin. And she managed to get herself pregnant."

In other circumstances, her last line would've been funny, one of those lines that deflect responsibility. She managed to get herself pregnant. Jack, of course, had had nothing to do with it. A poor passive figure and no more.

"That's why I'm here tonight."

"I guess I don't understand, Jean."

"He's been afraid to come out here since the last time they were together. And especially since she was killed."

"I guess I can understand that."

"Then after your confrontation with him. . . . he thinks you'll try to blame him for Sara's death. And for Egan's."

"Why would he have killed Egan?"

"Because Sara might have told him that she was pregnant with Jack's child."

"You did it again, huh?" I made it as soft as I could, as if I were talking to my kid sister.

"Did it again?"

"Forgave him."

"Oh. Yes. I see. Yes, I guess I did, didn't I?" Her gaze grew old and sad. "But it really wasn't his fault. She talked him into coming out here—he only did it because he was afraid she might have another one of her breakdowns—and when they got here, she seduced him. It really wasn't his fault, Sam."

We believe what we choose to believe, what we need to believe, however ludicrous that might be. If we couldn't lie to ourselves, we couldn't survive. But Jean's belief was extraordinary.

"He didn't kill them, Sam."

"All right."

"Do you believe me?"

"I'll try to."

"It's the truth, Sam."

"Where's your car?"

"My car? Why?"

"I thought I'd give you a ride to it."

She sipped some coffee. "I've still got things to do out here."

"Like what?"

"Making sure that she didn't leave anything behind out here. She was a true child, Sam. Beautiful, seductive, but a true child. Jack told me that she was always spilling her food on herself. He said he had to clean her up as if she were a three-year-old. He said that sometimes he had to clean her up the way he did our own daughter." She smiled. "I can hear all those Freudian red flags going up in your head, Sam. But it wasn't like that at all. She fooled people into thinking she was this little angel. Sweet and innocent, you know how teenage girls can fool people. And she seduced him. I'm sure she let *him* think he was seducing *her*. But it was really the other way around."

Hopeless. I couldn't take any more. I pitied her in a way I never wanted to pity anybody, in a condescending way, as if she were my house pet or a primate.

I stood up. "I need to go."

"Please don't get Jack involved in this."

"I'll try not to."

She flung off the cover and eased off the couch. She came to me and slid her arms around me. "Please, Sam. You two have never liked each other. But he'd never kill anybody. It just isn't in him. It really isn't. He's not perfect but none of us are, Sam. And Cliffie hates him. If you make Cliffie think that Jack's involved—"

I kissed her on the forehead. "'Night, Jean. I'll help you all I can."

"'Night, Sam." Then, "You ever wish we were kids again?"

"All the time."

Now that I knew my way, the walk back to my car was pleasant. Even the owls, grouchiest of all forest creatures, sounded friendly, and the tiny, bright earnest eyes observing me from the undergrowth seemed merry as Disney eyes.

I hoped to see Linda tonight. Or talk to her on the phone. At least for me, one sign of a good relationship is the ability to find yourself satisfied just to hear her voice. And the ability to spend an hour on the phone and have it go by like five minutes.

The door of my ragtop was open and it shouldn't have been open. Open maybe a quarter of an inch. Just enough to tell me that somebody had been here.

The back seat confirmed it. My briefcase was turned upside down and its contents dumped out. Somebody looking for something. I wondered if they'd found it.

Then I noticed the glove compartment door had been left open, too, everything it held spread out on the passenger's side of the front seat.

This could be random, of course. The tracks weren't that far away. A wandering hobo might have searched my car for money or anything he could hock. If that was the case, there was one disappointed hobo somewhere out there.

Just as I finished putting everything away in my briefcase, I heard the cry. I glanced around, not sure where it came from. Male, that was about all I knew for sure. And not too far away. Urgency, fear in the voice.

A second shout clarified his position. Within thirty seconds, I was back on the Comanche Trail, batting aside pine branches, shouting, "Where are you?" Already sweaty despite the chill, already anxious about this being some kind of trap. I just kept thinking about somebody tossing my car. Maybe he thought he could get more satisfaction out of dealing with me directly. I'd definitely eliminated the notion of a wandering hobo.

The oppressive smell of loam, the tripping-stumbling-scraping of trying to move through man-tall undergrowth. Tall as my five-five, anyway. He'd cried out again and this time I had a good sense of where he was.

I came into a tiny clearing, no bigger than a prison cell, and saw in the broken moonlight through the pines the six-foot rocky ravine below. At first I didn't recognize him. He was just some shadow lying back against the far side of the narrow ravine, pulling up the right leg of his jeans.

"Oh, shit, McCain, thank God."

It could only be Donny Hughes, teenage dipshit.

"You broke into my car, didn't you, Donny?"

"Exactly how do you break into a convertible when the top's already down, McCain? Now c'mon, help me. I think I broke my leg."

"What the hell were you looking for?"

"God, are you going to help me or not?"

"Not until you tell me what you were looking for?"

This sound of pain was dramatic as all hell. "C'mon, McCain. I can't stand up by myself. Didn't you have to take some kind of oath?"

"You're thinking of doctors and plumbers. Private investigators don't take oaths."

"Do you want to be responsible for my catching pneumonia and dying out here?"

"That'd make me popular with a lot of people in this town, Donny. Now why the hell were you rummaging around in my car?"

"I wanted to see what you had on her. She thinks you're trying to blame her for Sara and Egan."

"You mean Rita?"

The forest animals were enjoying this. It was TV for them. I could hear them scurrying, sliding, slithering to get closer. Two human beings talking. Life didn't get much better than that.

"I love her, McCain. I don't want to see her go to the gas chamber."

"That's one you don't have to worry about, Donny. In Iowa, we hang people. There isn't any gas chamber."

"Really? Hang people?"

"I don't like it, either. But that's what we do. No liquor by the drink because that's against God's law. But hang as many people as you want. That's just fine."

"Please, McCain. Please help me. I think gangrene's setting in."

"Listen, Donny, I've got a saw in my car. I'll go get it and we'll have that gangrene cut away in no time."

"McCain, I'm not kidding. I saw this Western once where the guy died of gangrene. He was foaming at the mouth and everything."

"That's rabies, Donny. Not gangrene."

"He had rabies? I didn't think cowboys could *get* rabies."

God only knew what that meant.

So I went down there, of course. And helped him, of course. And all the time I was doing my best to examine his leg he was bitching, of course. He was going to tell his dad how long I'd taken getting down here to help him. And his dad was going to sue me. And possibly give me rabies.

His leg was broken. I tried to feel sorry for Donny but you just can't. Maybe if he really did have rabies you could. But short of rabies, it was real, real hard to feel sorry for Donny under any circumstances.

The shin bone of his right leg was now snapped in two, the ragged upper part of it having torn through the flesh.

I said, "I have to say something, Donny. If my leg were busted like that, I'd do a lot more yelling than you have."

"Really?"

"Really. Let's get you to my car and get you to the hospital."

"Do you have a comb?"

That was Donny. A comb. Sure he was ugly, sure he was short, sure he was mouthy, but dammit he had great hair. Just like Elvis's. Just ask him.

His hot rod, he told me, was parked over near the ranger cabin.

"You know what he'll do, don't you, McCain?" he said.

"Who?"

"The park ranger."

"What'll he do?"

"Take my car for a spin."

"Yeah, I can see that. He's in his late forties, he lives in that small cabin with his wife and three kids, he's probably already in bed and asleep. And he's gonna get up and take your car for a spin."

"People resent the fact that my old man has all that money."

"No, they don't, Donny. They resent the fact that you're an asshole."

I hadn't meant to say it. Not consciously, anyway. It was like I was on automatic pilot except this was automatic insult.

"I'm sorry I said that, Donny."

"It's all right, McCain."

"No, it isn't, Donny. I apologize."

"I know what people think of me. The only one who really gets me is Rita. I bought her those boots, she wore them once, and now she says they hurt her feet and she can't wear them. That's the one that hurts, McCain. Rita."

"Gifts aren't going to get you anywhere with a girl like Rita, Donny."

"Then what the hell is, McCain? I've tried everything."

I helped him stand on his good leg. "If I had the answer, Donny, I'd be happily married and have three or four kids."

Getting up the side of the ravine was no fun. He wanted to do it on his own. I didn't blame him. Men should always try and look manly even if it means damn near killing themselves in the process.

Trip to the car, trip to the hospital, uneventful. He just talked about how much he loved Rita. It got tiresome. But then I remembered how tiresome I must have been back in the days when I still held out hope for me and the beautiful Pamela Forrest. Sometime, somewhere, everybody in his or her lifetime gets tiresome over somebody. That's as certain as death and taxes.

"I tried to make her jealous once," he said as we approached the hospital.

"What happened?"

"She told me she thought this other girl and I made a cute couple."

"I could see where that would piss you off."

"Then I tried not paying any attention to her."

"How'd that one go?"

"Well, after three weeks and four days, I went up to her said, 'Haven't you noticed that I haven't been paying any attention to you?' And she said, 'Oh, Donny, I'm sorry. I've just been so busy. So you really haven't been paying any attention to me?'"

"That must've hurt."

"That's when I started buying her stuff, McCain. I couldn't think of anything else to do."

As we were wheeling into the emergency end of the hospital, he said, "My folks think I'm a fool."

"You are a fool, Donny. And so am I and so is everybody else."

I took him inside and they got to work fixing up his broken leg. He was a lot more concerned about Rita than he was his broken bone.

Linda said, "I guess I'm pretty tired, Sam."

"So maybe I'd better not pop in, huh?"

A hesitation. "Sam."

There are a lot of ways you can say "Sam," but when it's said the way she had just said it, it's never good news.

"Yes."

"Sam, I—"

"You're not ready for this."

Another hesitation. "It's so confusing, Sam. And I feel I sort of—used you, you know."

"I like being used that way."

I was in a phone booth outside a noisy bar. The red neon of the place lent the night a gaudy humanity. People getting together to get drunk. Some staggering their way in, some staggering their way out. The happy ones were the ones who had girls to stagger out with him. If they had a girl, their grins made them look like kids, no matter how old they were.

"I just need some more time alone, I guess."

"I probably rushed things, Linda. I'm sorry."

"No, Sam. *I* rushed things. I had to find out how a man would react to—So I wouldn't think all men were like my ex-husband."

"I had a good time, Linda. I hope I can see you again."

"There's this shrink I see in Iowa City. I think I need to start seeing her again. I guess she's an expert at dealing with women who've had—you know, the kind of operation I've had. And I'm not going to drink, either. Liquor just confuses me." Then, "I'm really sorry, Sam. If it were some other time in my life—" Then, "G'night, Sam."

I drove around. I couldn't tell you where. I wasn't in love with her. That wasn't it. But it had felt good to be with her. Dating around had turned me into a pretty superficial guy. You said what you were expected to say on dates. There wasn't much genuine contact. But with Linda—

Easy for me to say, I finally realized as I slipped into bed that night. She's the one with the mastectomy. She's the one who has to beat the cancer odds. All I have to do is show up on dates wearing clean underwear.

TWENTY-TWO

I SLEPT. IT WAS escape sleep. Sometimes you sleep because you're tired, sometimes you sleep because you're bored. I slept because I didn't want to think anymore. Not about three murders, not about Linda.

In the morning I got up and burned myself a decent breakfast, showered, got into a fresh suit and tie, and got to the office half an hour earlier than usual.

Molly came along soon after.

God had sent her from on high. She'd brought two cardboard containers of steaming hot coffee from the café down the street.

"I just thought you might like some coffee."

She waited patiently while I took a couple of calls from the courthouse about two of my trials being postponed. She looked wan and worn but somehow that only enhanced her kind of coltish beauty.

When I was done, she said, "I just wanted to see how things were going."

"Not well. Mostly running into walls."

"God, that was terrible about Brenda."

"She saw something or she knew something."

"I'm not sure what you mean."

I took some coffee. "There's a possibility that one of her boyfriends killed her. Jealousy, something like that."

"She coached our softball team one summer. She was a nice woman. I didn't like to think of her sleeping around like that."

I smiled. "I hope you can always stay that forgiving and sweet, Molly. I really mean that, too." More coffee. "I wasn't running her down. I was just stating a fact. She did sleep around."

"Yeah, I guess she did," she said. "A little bit, anyway."

I liked that "a little bit, anyway." A last effort to save her friend's reputation.

"So, one of the men she slept with could have killed her, in which case her murder doesn't having any bearing on what I'm doing."

"Do you really think it was one of her men friends?" she said.

"Maybe—but I'm going to assume it was because of the timing. Sara dies, David dies, she dies. All in a very short period of time. There's some connection. It sure feels that way, anyway."

"David was in a pretty bad way the last time I saw him. He told me he was starting to steal money just so he could keep taking Sara out. It was funny—I really hated him for telling me something like that. But I couldn't help feeling sorry for him, either."

I'd been sitting back in my chair, the heel of my oxford on the edge of the desk. I sat up straight. "Stealing money? He told you that?"

"Yes. And I was scared for him. I told him he could go to jail. Maybe even prison if he kept doing it. But he said he couldn't stop himself."

"Did he say where he was stealing it from?"

"No. And I really didn't want to know anyway, Sam. I didn't want to get dragged into it."

"He was getting wilder and wilder."

"Yes, and drinking more and more. The last month or so, I rarely saw him sober."

"Do you have any sense of where he might have been getting his money?"

"No, I'm sorry, Sam, I really don't." Then, "I shouldn't say this but Sara wasn't a very nice girl, Sam. I know she had her troubles. But she shouldn't have led him on that way. She'd tell him she was still in love with this older man and could never love him, but then when he wouldn't call her for a few days, she'd call him. She'd always draw him back in. And he'd come running every time."

She daubed a tear with a fingertip. "I've got a whole day ahead of me? I didn't run my eye makeup, did I?"

"Nope. Beautiful as always."

"Oh, sure."

"You don't think you're beautiful?"

"I'm too gawky to be beautiful. I don't have any grace. But thanks for saying so." She gathered coat and purse and stood up and said, "I didn't know if that would help you or not. About him stealing money."

"It's sure worth following up."

I spent the rest of the morning working the telephone. I called the DX station, several clothing stores, and a custom car shop in Cedar Rapids that David always talked about. The money angle was something new. Maybe it wouldn't lead anywhere but it gave me a purpose and energy I hadn't been able to tune into this morning.

He owed nearly $10 at the DX station, nearly $250 at three different clothing shops, and had several small items on order from the custom car shop. The guy I spoke to said that David would have to pay cash before they'd give him the items. He said they'd given David credit once but that he'd been months overdue in paying it back.

Stolen money was my first surprise that morning. The second surprise was on the way as I was checking out David Egan's financial troubles.

I was on the phone with a client who'd been accused of stealing chickens from his neighbor. Though he wouldn't admit he'd done it, he did say that he was sure his neighbor had been stealing chickens from *him*. I wondered if Oliver Wendell Holmes had ever handled a chicken-stealing case. I was just hanging up when my office door opened and Jean Coyle came in.

Tear-reddened eyes. A trembling left hand. A cigarette in the right hand. A forlorn elegance as she sat in the chair and listened to me wind things up with my client. All of a sudden I didn't have much interest in chicken rustling, not that I had all that much in the beginning.

She took many, many drags on her cigarette, not inhaling a one of them.

As soon as I hung up, she waved her cigarette in the air and said, "This is for dramatic effect. I don't even know how to smoke these things."

"The red eyes are all you need for dramatic effect. Why don't you put it out?"

I pushed the ashtray across the desk. She was, as always, the compleat suburban house mistress. A long gray coat of suede and leather patches, a starched white collar on her blouse, and an impeccable hairstyle.

After punishing her cigarette several times over, she finally got every tiny piece of flame out.

"You want to know how much I hated her?" Her voice wavered, went weak, came back strong in the same short question. "He—what's the phrase the kids use—knocked her up."

"He being—"

"—my husband, Jack."

"And she being—"

"The recently deceased Sara Griffin." Then, "Is that bitchy enough for you? Talking about a poor dead girl like that?"

"Yeah. I heard."

I reached into my bottom drawer and hauled out a pint of Old Grandad. I shoved it across to her. She knew just what to do. Uncapped it, wiped off the neck with her palm, and took a swig a farmhand would have a hard time getting down.

"Mind if I keep this for a while?" she said.

"Be my guest."

"If I get drunk and try to seduce you, please say no."

"It just so happens I'm wearing my chastity belt." Then, "Could we go over this he-she business a little bit more?"

"He knocked her up."

"And you know this for sure?"

She snorted. "Are you kidding? The sonofabitch told me himself. He said when they make the autopsy public today, they'll announce she was pregnant." Then, "Will you handle my divorce for me?"

"Of course. If you're sure that's what you want."

"If I'm sure that's what I want? My God, Sam, how could I live with a man like that? He promised that first time they had an affair that it was all over. Then—and he told me this, too—he started seeing her again three months ago. And he got her pregnant. It just all came down on me when she was killed. That I'm all tied up in this somehow." She leaned over toward the bottle. "Do I want another drink?"

"Probably not."

"You're always so damned sensible."

"Me? Are you kidding?"

"Well, you're a lot more sensible than I'm being at the moment, anyway."

I said, "I'm going to ask you a question and you're probably going to hate me for it."

"You're going to ask me if he killed her."

"Yes."

"I've thought about it ever since last night. He says he didn't, of course." She was starting to be her usual proper self. The self I liked because she was so elegant to watch. Proper doesn't have to be stuffy. "He made a good case for himself."

"That being?"

"That being, say he did kill Sara Griffin. Why would he kill Egan and Brenda?"

I took a swig myself. "That's where I'm hung up, too. I'm trying to figure out what connects them."

"That's where I keep ending up, too. He wouldn't have any reason to kill them, too. But I hear Cliffie is promoting the idea that one of Brenda's lovers killed her and that Egan killed himself."

"Good old Cliffie."

She said, "Maybe I'd just have one more small drink." I pushed the pint back over to her. She took a mincing little drink. "I'm terrible."

"Yes, Jean, you are terrible. Right up there with Hitler and Rasputin."

"I mean wanting my own husband to be charged with murder. I didn't know I had that kind of spite in me. It's not the sort of thing you want to know about yourself. I mean, it's so selfish to even *think* about. My Lord, think of our girls. It would destroy their lives." Then, "But I am going to divorce him."

"Good."

"He's got a lot of money stashed away in secret places."

"We'll find it."

"May I come back and talk to you about it when I'm not in such a bitchy mood?"

"Sure. Anytime you want to."

When she stood up, she consciously composed herself, straightened coat, collar, touched hair, arranged her purse strap just so over her shoulder. "You probably get a lot of hysterical women in here."

"You're not hysterical. Given what you just found out, you were damned well appropriate."

"Now there's a nice word to save face with. 'Appropriate.' I was 'appropriate' all the way down here." She smiled for the first time. "I was 'appropriate' when I was going seventy-five miles an hour in a thirty-five zone; and I was 'appropriate' when I laid on my horn because some old geezer was doing twenty and I couldn't get around him. And I was especially 'appropriate' when I was guzzling your bourbon like a sailor on shore leave." She laughed. "Thanks for letting me in on that word. 'Appropriate.' I have a feeling I'll be using that a lot now."

She went to the door, turned and said, "Thanks, Sam," and was gone.

TWENTY-THREE

I HAD A COURT case in the afternoon. Divorce. Neither party especially likable. But their little girl was sweet and sad. And neither parent seemed to notice. The kid would lose no matter which parent got custody. They'd both been unfaithful, verbally abusive, and even treacherous to each other. I pretended to be on the side of my male client but it wasn't easy. The judge, the patron saint of all grumpy old men who existed on whiskey and Tums, favored the lady. So would I if I'd been looking only at her breasts.

After court, I cashed some client checks at the bank and then went around paying off my bills at the grocery store, the record shop, and the gas station.

Back at the office, Jamie and Carrie were still working on refiling everything.

Correction: Carrie was still working on the filing. Jamie was in the john and didn't appear for fifteen minutes after I got there.

"See," she said to Carrie, "you hardly notice them, they look so natural."

She referred to the huge fanlike false eyelashes she wore. They gave her eyes that feral and cunning look of the B-girls you meet in some of Chicago's seamier bars. Not that I've had experience with those girls, personally.

I returned the calls waiting for me. I noticed that the notes on the call slips were filled out in a neat, easily readable hand and that the descriptions were grammatical and informative.

I said, "Who took all these messages?"

Carrie continued to file, said nothing. Jamie was perched on her desk chair, her compact out, examining her new three-pound eyelashes in the compact mirror. She didn't shift her gaze but she did say, "Don't be too hard on her, Mr. C. This was the first time she took your calls. I would've done it but I have to save my voice."

"Save your voice? What for?"

"I'm making Turk take me to this hootenanny in Iowa City tonight. Twelve different folk singers. He doesn't want to go because his uncle told him that all folk singers are perverts and communists."

"Who's his uncle? J. Edgar Hoover?"

Jamie, of course, didn't get the joke. But Carrie did. She laughed most pleasantly. Jamie gave her cousin a quizzical look.

I said, "I still don't get why you have to save your voice?"

"Because I like to sing along. I don't want my voice to be all scratchy. In fact, I shouldn't even be talking now."

I glanced at Carrie, expecting her to let me know somehow that she realized how silly if—I have to admit it—sweet Jamie is. But she turned back to her filing work quickly.

I made some more phone calls. I did some more paperwork.

"Would you like some coffee, Mr. McCain?" Carrie said after a while.

"Golly, Carrie, I told you to call him Mr. C. Right, Mr. C?"

"I don't know him as well as you do, Jamie, so I think I'll just stick to Mr. McCain."

"She's kind of square, Mr. C. But she's real nice."

Jamie went back to her eyebrows.

"I made some fresh," Carrie said. "I hope you don't mind."

I generally drink only a single morning cup of the coffee I make here at the office. The rest I inflict on clients.

I didn't want to insult her, so I said, "Sure. I'll take a cup." Not expecting much. She poured, brought it over. I raised the cup, drank it. "This is really good."

"Thank you."

I didn't want get too effusive. Eventually even Jamie was going to figure out that her cousin was a much better worker than she was. I went back to work. Five o'clock was coming on.

When the phone rang, Carrie picked it up and said, "This is Mr. McCain's law office. How may I help you?"

My Lord. It was a bit on the formal side, her greeting, but she had a crisp, smart phone voice and sounded pretty damned big- city.

"Oh, yes, your honor, he's right here," Carrie said.

She handed the receiver to me.

Judge Esme Anne Whitney said, "My God, McCain, a secretary who speaks English? What did you do, kidnap her? What happened to that busty little idiot who's always fornicating with that juvenile delinquent boyfriend of hers?"

"I assume you have a serious question for me."

"Indeed, I do. When in the hell are you going to wrap this thing up? If one more person says to me that Egan killed poor Sara Griffin and then committed suicide—"

"That's when you explain to them that Cliffie's theory doesn't make any sense. If Egan wanted to kill himself, he sure wouldn't have cut his own brake line. He might have driven off the edge of the cliff that way. But cut his brake line? What's the sense of that?"

"In other words, you haven't found the killer yet."

"In other words, I'm working on it."

"I'm having a small dinner party at my house tonight. I'd love to tell everybody that once again I've shown up Cliffie for the boob he is."

I sighed. "I don't think this is the kind of thing that works on a timetable like that."

"Well, if it isn't," she said in her most imperious tone of voice, "it should be."

And with that we—actually, she—hung up.

When I turned my attention to the girls again, Jamie was holding up a doe-colored brushed leather flat for Carrie to see.

"I have to wear these tonight," Jamie said in a voice only a teenage girl could muster, "it's the only thing I have that goes with this sweater-and-skirt outfit I bought."

"What's the matter with it?" I said.

"She picked up something on the street," Carrie said, "some kind of stain."

"Here, let me see it."

The stain ran along the bottom side of the shoe, all the way to the toe, where it splayed wide. The discoloration was obvious. She'd stepped in some kind of liquid chemical, apparently, maybe an insecticide the city had sprayed on the sidewalks.

"What'm I going to do?" Jamie said. The last act of Hamlet couldn't hold any more drama than this moment with the shoe.

I ate in a diner that night and pretended I was in an Edward Hopper painting. Most of the customers were solitary work-ingmen. In a doctor's office you wonder what sort of malady the other patients are suffering from. In a diner you wonder what sort of fractured life the customers are suffering from. At supper-time in a small town most men are home with their families. What about these men? Why were they all here?

Then we had one of those charged communal male moments when a pretty redhead came in and sat down and ordered a cheeseburger and a Pepsi. A depth charge of feeling and need had awakened us. The isolated looks of the men at the U-shaped counter changed into interested, lively looks. The girl had redeemed us all, at least for a few minutes. She'd reacquainted some of us with our lust. For the more romantic, including me, she'd stirred not only lust but that great longing for something resembling true love. She was nice enough to bless each of us with her version of a papal smile (*Bless you, my horny lost children*) and to stretch a little bit every once in a while so we could see the lift of her small but lovely breasts.

She ate quickly. Probably had a date. We all took turns pretending not to watch her. And then she stood up.

She paid her bill and turned toward the door, which she got halfway open before stumbling. It's something we all do, unless we're Fred Astaire or Gene Kelly. But usually nothing happens. We right ourselves and continue on stumbling through.

Then it happened.

First, her entire left side sank down a couple of inches. And then her sweet bow-shaped mouth opened to let out a small sharp cry of pain.

Damned near every one of us came off our counter stools.

What had happened was that she'd not only twisted her ankle, she'd also snapped off the heel of her pump.

We all pushed and shoved to be the one who got to help her back to her seat. The Three Stooges would have been proud of the melee we created. Even with her pain she was able to smile at what dopes men were.

The waitress poured her a free cup of coffee. A man who claimed to have been a medic in the navy had the pleasure of feeling up the ankle she'd turned. Another man offered to drive her to the hospital. Apparently he thought she was in need of some heavy-duty surgery. You never can tell about sprained ankles. One minute the person's fine and dandy; the next minute there they are, laid out on the floor, waiting for a funeral home director to stick a red rose in their pale dead fingers. Those darned sprained ankles.

I got out of there and drove around for a time, melancholy as always at dusk. Mostly I thought of Linda and how attached I felt to her after only a few dates. But that appeared to be another brief relationship in a life of brief relationships.

And then I had a thought I should have had some time ago. You don't need to hit me over the head with a board. You need to hit me over the head with a board and an anvil.

Shoes.

The redhead in the diner had lost her heel. Jamie had soiled her brushed leather flat.

And Rita Scully had stains on her new desert boots that could easily have come from oil.

Rita knew where Egan kept his car in his aunts' backyard. Easy enough to sneak in there and cut the brake line, late on some moonless night.

But the ground was soaked with oil from Egan working on his car all the time.

A quick way to stain a brand new pair of light-colored desert boots.

The stables were closed for the night. Moonlight traced the two-story stucco house where the Scullys lived. The light in the windows looked warm and comfortable against the autumn night. The stars sent me all the usual greetings and warnings and reassurances that I'd never been able to understand. There'd be frost for sure in a few hours.

I parked on the gravel road on the hill below the stables. I went down to a narrow dry creek then up a burr-filled hillside to a barbed-wire fence that just might have been as old as I was.

Even from here I could smell the horse manure and the hay from the barn. The business office, which is where I wanted to go, was dark. Probably locked. Good thing a client of mine, headed back to prison and in no need of them, had given me his burglary tools. Even so, he still owed me $350, which I would see just about the time we put a man or woman on Pluto.

A few minutes later, I joined the stained shoe club. I stepped in horseshit so fresh I actually skidded half a foot or so on it. It was sort of like ice skating, sort of.

I'd had this fear that the horses would hear me or smell me or take some kind of psychic notice of me and start whinnying their asses off. Apparently, they were all watching TV or reading because they didn't so much as whimper as I crossed in front of the barn doors.

I ducked behind the office and then peeked out again at the lighted windows. I couldn't see any shadow figures moving behind the curtains but I could hear a burst of laughter and then what sounded like somebody talking loudly to a person up the inside stairs.

I spent a minute trying to get the crap off my shoe by running it through a patch of grass. I'm not sure it helped much but it made me feel in control of the situation—take that, horseshit—and that's all that matters.

The only tense moment was getting the door open. I have six picks and three keys. And of course the one I wanted was the last one I tried. I kept glancing up at the house. Nobody seemed to be peering out.

I got the door open, feeling pretty damned clever, and then I half jumped inside. I hadn't taken into account what the effect of horse poop could have on the sole of an oxford when it came in contact with a linoleum floor.

Before I could get the door closed, which would at least have muffled the sound, I slid and tripped forward, cartwheeling my arms as I slammed into the side of a tall metal storage cabinet, the one next to where Rita kept all her shoes and boots lined up. I also said a dirty word. Well, I didn't *say* a dirty word. I *shouted* a dirty word.

And then I held my breath, like a tot who can't have another piece of cake and so decides to take his own life right in front of his mommy and show her, by God, what happens to mean, selfish women like her.

Oh, did I hold my breath.

I expected Mr. Scully to come running out here with a couple of flame-throwers and a boxful of grenades. Cliffie would love this, me being caught breaking into some place with burglary tools. And the judge would fire me for sure.

Nothing happened.

I can't say I was disappointed but I was surprised. The house wasn't that far away. Surely they must have heard—

But apparently not.

Now I needed to move and move quickly. I dug out the tiny flashlight I carry with me to use in such circumstances—and to check out the tonsils of the girls I date when they say they're not feeling well and guess they'll go home early—and the shoes and boots weren't there.

A few minutes later, I was completing my search of the office when somebody snapped the ceiling light on.

"I could shoot you and get away with it, you know that, don't you?"

I turned and looked at Rita Scully. "Three murders aren't enough, Rita?"

"Oh, shit, McCain. Give it a rest."

She came in, walked over to her desk, sat down, and said, "How the hell'd you get in here?"

"Where are the boots?"

"What boots?"

"The boots that were lined up against the wall over there."

"I took them up to the house."

"Why?"

"Why? What difference does it make to you?"

"A lot of difference. Now tell me why you took those boots up to the house."

"You are one goofy sonofabitch, you know that?"

"The desert boots Donny Hughes bought you. Those are the ones I want to see."

"The desert—" She stopped herself and a cold, superior smile made her particular kind of loveliness hard and mean. "You mean these?"

She pushed back from the desk in her chair and then set both of her desert boots on her desk. "Pretty exciting boots, huh?"

"I thought they were too small for you."

"My dad let me use these stretchers he had. That helped a lot." She waggled one of the boots at me. "Pretty exciting, huh, McCain?"

I peered down at it. "Oil stain."

"Exactly right. If this were a game show, you'd win a refrigerator."

"You snuck over there, didn't you?"

"Snuck over where?"

"Snuck over to Egan's late at night and cut his brake line and got your boots all oily doing it."

"God, McCain, you're such a moron, I can't believe it. You actually think I murdered David and those two others?"

"You've got oil on your shoes."

"And you've got rocks in your head."

I wasn't sure at first what she slipped from the pocket of her red Western shirt. It was a cigarette and somehow not a cigarette.

When I realized what it was, and what she was going to do with it, I thought that it looked wrong. She shouldn't be wearing Western gear. She should be in black, a beatnik girl in a shabby, crowded apartment where cool jazz fought pretentious conversations for domination in the room.

But it didn't seem to bother her. She was Annie Toke-ly of the West. She put the reefer in her lips and lit up. Then she closed her eyes and let the magic do its work. The smell was, as always, sweet and stark, and more than a little scary. An attorney caught in a place where marijuana was being smoked would lose his ticket, even if he could prove that he hadn't actually smoked any himself.

She took two long hits. "I get pretty frisky when I smoke this reefer, McCain." She giggled. It was a marijuana giggle, friendly as a puppy and just a wee bit daft. "If I don't keep smoking this stuff, all I do is lie on my bed and cry about David. Excuse me."

She took two more long hits.

"Your folks know you smoke this?"

She was holding it in her lungs and didn't want to exhale. She shook her head. When she exhaled, she said, "Are you kidding? My dad'd take a riding crop to me." Then, "I didn't kill him. Or any of them."

"Then who did?"

"Isn't that supposed to be your job?"

"I'm always up for a little help."

"Just a sec."

Another deep inhalation.

The exhalation came in a ragged burst.

"Guess who I called today, McCain?"

"Who?"

"Molly."

"For what?"

"I figured now was the time to be friends again. We're both mourning David. We should comfort each other."

"What'd she say?"

Sly smile. "She hung up on me. But that's Molly. Always takes awhile to bring her around."

"She's a nice kid."

"And I'm not, I suppose?"

She didn't wait for my answer. She took another deep hit. The reefer was burning to ash quickly.

"You really want me to answer that?"

She looked as if she were inhaling helium, the way her head seemed to rise and swell as she held the smoke deep in her lungs. Then the explosion.

"I don't sleep around, McCain. David's the only guy I ever slept with, in fact. I don't drink much. I go to church. I try to help people whenever I can. You seem to think I'm some kind of slut."

"Molly's under the impression that you were bad for Egan."

"Molly's under the impression that everybody was bad for David—except her, of course."

"Did you get Egan started on marijuana or the other way around?"

But she was taking the last drag on the reefer. All the Iowa City and Chicago hipster parties I'd touristed my way through came back. I swear I could hear a couple of sexy Northwestern coeds discussing Sartre.

Boom. She exhaled.

"You didn't know your client very well, McCain."

"Meaning what?"

"His asthma. And all his allergies. He tried smoking reefers a couple of times and his glands swelled up on him and he had this miserable asthma attack. He didn't like it when I smoked grass. He said it made me too crazy. He took a whole bunch of my joints and kept them in his room. He'd only let me smoke one a week. He told me he got his aunts to try it once. Thought it'd be funny. They loved it." The sly smile again. "Be sure and tell Molly that, will you? That I'm not some slut? That I didn't seduce him into drugs or anything? I really think now is a good time to be friends again. She was my best friend for ten years. We used to trade dolls and clothes and do overnights all the time. Even when I hated her for David, I missed her. I couldn't talk to anybody—not even David—the way I used to talk to her."

She snubbed out the reefer between thumb and forefinger and popped it into her mouth the way she would a vitamin pill.

"Thrifty girl," she said, after swallowing it. "I always eat the roach. Why waste it?" Then, "I can see you now." She stumbled over her words. The reefer was taking effect. "Racing out here in your deerstalker cap. Thinking you had me because of the oil stain on my desert boots." The marijuana giggle again. "Poor McCain." Her eyes gleamed merrily. "A wasted trip."

"Not at all," I said, standing up. "You told me something important that I needed to know." Then, "I've got a lot of horse-shit on my shoe."

"Occupational hazard around here."

"There a hose anywhere I could wash it off? I've got one more stop to make tonight."

"East side of the barn there's a hose we use for the water trough. So where's this next stop of yours, anyway?"

"That's for me to know and you to find out."

Another giggle. "God, I haven't heard that since fourth grade."

She shrugged. "I don't really give a shit where you're going, anyway." She pulled out the center drawer of the desk and came up with a Snickers, ripping the wrapper off with spectacular ferocity. "Boy, when I get like this, McCain, high and all like this, I'll bet I could eat twenty of these things in a row and not miss a beat. I might puke somewhere along the line but I'd go right back to eating if I did."

Gone gone gone, she was.

Gone gone gone.

"Tell Molly I love her, McCain."

"I'll tell her," I said, starting for the door.

Giggle giggle. "And tell her that I'd like to trade dolls again."

A couple of minutes later, I used the hose to wash away the horse feces and then made my way carefully to my car.

This time I used the driveway instead of the ravine and the grassy hill.

TWENTY-FOUR

IT WAS THE WORLD of my grandfather and grandmother. The world of all those long-ago folks who'd fled their beloved land because it no longer fed or tolerated them. And so they came to the new country and mixed old with new—supermarkets and cars with fins and Joe McCarthy with crucifix and holy Mary and holy water to be sure; and brogues and lilts and song in their voices, and joy and fear and resentment and great vast hope in their eyes. The tiny old women at daily mass, their heads covered in cheap faded scarves; the whiskey-faced, knuckle-swollen union leaders shouting at the scabs who'd crossed the picket line; and the sweet, young, skinny-legged girls in their school uniforms up in the choir loft intoxicated by the scent of incense and the sound of the bells ringing out in the belfry as they had in Belfast and Donegal and Kerry. And now they had Bing Crosby and his songs from the old country on their phonographs, and Jackie Gleason and Bishop Sheen on their televisions, and so many sports figures they were uncountable. And one of them, the son of a bootlegger, might soon become president—imagine that, president—of the entire country. Old and new.

I felt the crush of all that history as I heard light footsteps beyond the door. And felt it still as the porch light came on in the smoky autumn night. And there stood Amy Kelly.

"Why, hello, Sam. You timed it just right. Emma made a cake this afternoon. C'mon in."

I went inside and everything had changed. It was no longer a cozy, bright little home. I'd never noticed before how long and dark the shadows were, how stained the wallpaper was, how threadbare the area rugs looked. And how lumpy and beaten the furnishings were.

Most of all, their faces had changed. Emma came in and stood next to Amy. And their faces were grotesque. Not in the monster-movie way but in the way their eyes regarded me—cold, alien eyes—these saintly women who were not saintly at all.

They tried, of course, to pretend we were still living inside that Norman Rockwell painting this house and these women had always inhabited. To those who didn't really know them, anyway. Including me.

Emma, as you would expect, sensed my real business here long before her sister did.

Amy said, "Would you like a couple spoons of ice cream with your cake, Sam? It's chocolate cake. And vanilla ice cream."

Emma said, in a voice both strained and harsh, "He isn't here for cake and ice cream, sister. Now please be quiet."

Amy started to say something else—she looked shocked at the sudden change in her sister's mood—but her sister said, "Go upstairs, Amy."

"What? What are you talking about?"

"I said to go upstairs." She grabbed Amy's arm with her left hand and gave her a little push on the back with her right. "Go upstairs now and play some music on the radio in your room. I want to hear that music and want you in your room."

Amy turned to me for explanation and support. "What's going on here, Sam?"

"I think Emma's right, Amy. Why don't you go upstairs?"

I'd wondered if it had been both of them. Now I knew better.

Amy started reluctantly, almost as if she'd forgotten how to walk, to the staircase.

"Don't you think one of you owes me an explanation? This is my house, too, you know."

"Get up there, sister. And no more dawdling."

The child had been ordered, once and for all, to her room. The child was smart enough, finally, to go.

She put a hand on the banister, swept her housedress about her as if she were Scarlett O'Hara, and disappeared on the second tier of the stairway.

"Why don't we sit in the kitchen and drink a little Irish coffee?" She sounded friendlier now. Amy's leaving had apparently freed her somehow.

And so we did.

"You want a full shot in it?"

"Half," I said. "I'm no drinker."

She smiled. "Neither am I. Not until lately, anyway." For the first time I heard sorrow and perhaps fear in her voice. "But then everything's changed now, hasn't it?" She put a full shot in her coffee.

We sat at a small table that smelled of its oilcloth covering. The ancient refrigerator throbbed. The faucet dripped. The Jesus of the kitchen lithograph looked just as sad as I felt.

"You know what's funny?"

"What?"

"I never liked him."

"That surprises me."

"Right from the start he was moody and angry and belligerent.

And he started stealing from us when he wasn't even quite seven years old. I even thought of sending him to an orphanage—Lord knows we didn't have the money to send him to some private school—but Amy wouldn't hear of it. He was Amy's boy. No matter what he did, she found some way of excusing it. If I was hard with him, she'd sneak into his room and give him money, to make him feel better. She never saw the way he used her. So she let him get away with everything."

I lit a cigarette. The kitchen had never seemed this small, this oppressive before. I wondered if it felt the same way to her.

Emma smiled as radio music came on upstairs. Dance band music from the thirties. "Poor Amy. I treat her so bad sometimes."

"I've been trying to put this together, Emma. From what you just told me, I can see why you have lost your temper with David. But why Sara?"

"You're not that good at it, Sam. David killed Sara, I didn't. Right in the backyard here. They'd been upstairs arguing for half an hour at least. Her parents thought she was home. But she snuck out and came over here. David said they were going out. She looked very embarrassed about all the arguing. He killed her in the car right out there in the backyard, like I said. I watched him put her in the trunk. When he came home that night, I told him I was going to the police. I made him tell me everything. He put her body in the Coyles' gazebo so Cliffie would think that Jack Coyle had killed her. I guess they'd been having some kind of unholy affair—Lord, a man of that age. Then after he dumped the body, he tore out to Brenda's house. She was drunk, of course. He'd convinced her that he'd been there for an hour longer than he actually was. He told me that he was going to pretend to save her reputation by not telling Cliffie who he'd been with. Then at the last minute, he'd tell Cliffie her name and he'd have his alibi."

"Then you went ahead and cut his brake line."

She sighed. Dropped her eyes to the worked and wrinkled hands that surrounded her coffee cup. "I'm going to have a hard time telling Father Laymon that in confession."

"And then Brenda," I said quietly.

A sip of her coffee. A hand at the back of her neck, as if she were having pain. And a deep ragged sigh.

"She wanted money to leave her husband—just run out on him. She wanted two thousand dollars from me. Can you imagine that? Where would somebody like me get two thousand dollars?"

"She was blackmailing you?"

"Trying to. She called me three different times. She was drunker every time she called. She'd figured out that David had tricked her into giving him an alibi. She said that the way things stood, a lot of people thought David had just committed suicide. That he didn't have nerve enough to do it the way most people do. So he cut his brake line. He wouldn't know when or where or how it would happen. He'd just get in a drag race and—" She raised her gaze to me directly. "She was so miserable, I probably did her a favor. That's a horrible thing to say. But it's true. I don't think much of her husband—the way he's always swaggering around like he's still the big sports hero—but he deserved a better wife than her. I almost felt sorry for her."

Her gaze shifted past me and she smiled then at something I couldn't see. "You're getting sneaky in your old age, sister."

I turned and saw Amy in the doorway. In little more than a whisper, she said, "You should've talked to me, Emma. I could've helped you. I'd never desert you, Emma. I want to go where you go."

Just before she moved away from the kitchen door, sobbing, everything in the house took on its old, comfortable self. I liked all the old mismatched furnishings, and the thrum of that damned refrigerator motor, and the smell of the oilcloth.

We listened as Amy, still sobbing, ran up the stairs, slamming her door when she reached her room.

"She's never going to forgive me, Sam."

"Maybe never forgive you. But she'll understand you. Someday."

"At my age, I don't have a lot of somedays left, Sam."

I let her cry for a while and then I went around the table and raised her to her feet and took her in my arms. She had the bones of old age, so fragile and yet so sharp, and flesh that was dried freckled tissue covering the lean meat of mortality.

I sat down in her chair and put her on my lap and said, "We're going to figure out how to handle Cliffie tomorrow morning when I take you in. And then we're going to get you the best criminal lawyer in the state, all right?"

And when she raised her ancient face, she was no longer monster or ghoul, but a young Irish girl again—for just that moment I saw the girl she'd been, Easter hat and Christmas dress and first-date hair ribbon—and when I held her this time, I was holding all those years, an entire life, in my arms and I felt her heartbeat slow and the nervous spasm in her left arm cease and heard her crying become little more than sniffles.

She said, "Will you go talk to Amy for me, Sam? I'd really appreciate it."

TWENTY-FIVE

I DROVE AROUND AND then I didn't drive around, sitting in a tavern where the gents along the bar were arguing Kennedy-Nixon, coming up in two weeks, and then I drove around again but not for long because I just kept thinking of Amy sobbing, "If our father ever knew what his daughter did—I'm so glad my folks are dead and don't have to see this. And killing poor David." And finally, realizing for the first time the practical implications of this terrible night: "Who'll I live with now, Sam? Emma's my whole life, my whole life."

The lights shouldn't have been turned on. Neither should the TV. My first thought was a burglar of some kind, but who'd burgle my little apartment?

Or maybe a dissatisfied client or his emissary. You lose a trial, sometimes they have kin gunning for you. Hell, if a plotline like that is good enough for *Gunsmoke*, it's good enough for Black River Falls.

I saw her through the window in the door. All comfy-cozy on the couch. Tasha, Crystal, and Tess all pushed tight against her at various points in her body.

She looked like she belonged there.

When she heard my key in the door, she jumped up and rushed toward me.

"I've really been worried about you. Mrs. Goldman let me in again. She's sure a nice woman."

"She sure is."

I came in. Took off my suitcoat, balled it, and tossed it for two points on the chair. "Needs to be dry-cleaned, anyway."

"Oh."

"I thought maybe you were a burglar."

"I don't think I could ever be anything as exciting as a burglar. And besides, I'm very happy being a nurse."

"You sure are pretty."

"I've missed you, Sam. I'm just confused about everything."

"Me, too."

We still weren't touching in any way. We were maybe half a foot apart. The cats were on the couch, watching us. They wanted some action.

"Sam, have you ever just slept with a woman? No going all the way, I mean?"

"Honest?"

"Honest."

"I've tried."

"It didn't work?"

"I don't think she really wanted it to work and I know I didn't want it to work."

"Oh."

"But if I really made my mind up—"

"It'd be putting a lot of pressure on you—"

"I've got the shower standing close by."

She grinned. "That'd be a help. You have any handcuffs?"

"Sorry, all out. Just leg irons."

"Well, that could be interesting."

"I could loan you my gun. You could pistol whip me."

Half seriously, she said, "Well, it was a stupid idea, I guess."

"Aw, let's give it a try."

"You won't try—"

"We'll do whatever you want. Or don't want."

"We have to have strict rules, though."

"How strict? Is kissing allowed?"

"I suppose kissing would be all right."

"Sort of pressing against each other. Would that be all right?"

"I suppose sort of pressing against each other would be all right, too, if it was just sort of."

"Saying that I've missed you and I don't know where this is going but I sure do like you? Would that be all right?"

"That'd be best of all, Sam."

"Well, how about if we start the kissing part just standing right here in the middle of the floor?"

"Sometimes that's the best place of all, Sam. Right here in the middle of the floor."

"The good old middle of the floor," I said. "The good old middle of the floor."

TWENTY-SIX

THE CALL CAME AT 3:37 A.M. according to the glowing
face of my nightstand clock.

Judge Whitney. Not only sober. Alarmed.

"Did Cliffie just call you?"

"No."

It wasn't exactly a lie. The phone had rung. I just decided not
to answer it. I didn't want to go down and bail somebody out.
But this time the phone woke Linda first and she said, ever the
responsible nurse, "You'd better get it, Sam. It could be important this hour of the night."

So I'd lifted the receiver and put it to my ear and listened to the
judge and said, "So what did Cliffie want?"

"Then you haven't heard?"

"Heard what?"

And then she said it: "Emma Kelly killed her sister tonight.
And then killed herself. I imagine she didn't have a hard time
finding a weapon. Her father was a gunsmith, you know."

I must have made some kind of startled sound, because Linda
sat up in bed and turned on the reading lamp.

All I could think of was sad, lost Amy in the doorway of their kitchen saying, *I want to go where you go*. I wondered if she'd begged Emma to kill her, too. A mortal sin, to be sure, but Amy would likely commit it to be with her sister.

"Did you hear what I said, McCain?"

"Yeah," I said, "yeah, I heard all right."

I sat silent on the edge of the bed for a long, long time, smoking one cigarette after another. Linda knew not to ask me about it.

After a while she came over and sat down on the bed next to me and put an arm around my shoulder. "Maybe I'd better go, Sam."

I came out of my silence and looked at her and said, "I'll give you a dollar if you'll stay."

She smiled. "How about two dollars?"

She was kind enough and smart enough to take me in her arms and just hold me for a long and silent time.